I Blame Myself

But Also You

and other stories

Spencer Fleury

Earlier versions of some of the stories in this collection have previously appeared in the following publications:

"The Insomniac Traveler's Guide to the Lost Pyramids of Quartzsite, Arizona": *Big Muddy*, 2019
"Tube Man": *Disclaimer*, 2016
"Singapore Song": *The Apalachee Review*, 2020
"When the Drought Finally Ends": *The Collapsar*, 2016
"Hugo": *Blunderbuss*, 2014
"Fantastic Atlas": *Ascent*, 2018
"Controlled Descent": *Ascent*, 2019
"Headbangers' Ball": *Permafrost*, 2019
"Fancy Gap": *Word Riot*, 2014

ISBN: 979-8-9903240-8-4

Published July 2024 by Malarkey Books

Cover design by David Wojciechowski

malarkeybooks.com

Contents

I Blame Myself But Also You

The man on the scooter handled his ride in an unsteady fashion, wobbling across the dashed yellow center line and into Lindsay's lane, heading directly for her. At that moment, her six-year-old Jetta was the only car in the eastbound lane, and they were still about a block and a half apart.

She thought the man might be drunk, and then immediately chastised herself for jumping to such an uncharitable conclusion about someone she didn't even know. He might be new at this.

That could also explain why he wore no helmet.

She slowed down, to about twenty miles an hour, to give him plenty of time to recover and get back across the center line.

But the man's course did not waver. He lined up along the exact center of Lindsay's lane, as if he was aiming for her in particular. She slowed down again, almost to a full stop this time. The man kept coming. Within seconds his scooter was just yards away from her car, and by now she was going too slowly to maneuver out of his way. She didn't know what else to do, so she leaned on her horn, but he just lowered his head, raised his body slightly on his scooter, and speeded up.

There could be no doubt about it now. He meant to ram her.

Maybe she could throw the car into reverse and back away from this lunatic. She looked in the rearview mirror, saw it was clear, but just as she reached for the gearshift knob, she heard the crunch of folding metal and cracking plastic and felt the car shudder backward from the impact of the scooter smashing into her hood.

Then she heard a different, wetter sort of crunch, this one made by the cracking of ribs and the snapping of a spine in a body that had just been pitched over the top of her car to a landing spot fifteen feet behind it.

Oh shit, Lindsay thought. *My car. That man. My insurance.* And she scolded herself again, this time for thinking of something as heartlessly reasonable as car insurance in a moment like this, a moment in which a man may have just died because she couldn't get out of his way fast enough.

She forced herself to look in the rearview again. The man lay in the middle of the street. He was still moving a little, but she couldn't tell if they were intentional gestures or just posthumous twitches.

Lindsay got out of her car and ran to him, even though she had no idea what she could possibly do to help. She crouched down next to the man and was shocked to discover that not only was he still alive, he was even still conscious. He looked up at her. His eyes were frantic and unfocused.

Not knowing what else to do, she took his hand. "Are you okay?" she asked. She knew that was the dumbest possible question she could have put to him just then. But she also knew she should say something, and she couldn't think of anything better.

"I thought for sure," he said between labored breaths, "that was gonna work."

"Why did you do that?"

"I flew," the man said. "Only a few seconds. But I was flying."

He seemed to be fading; she wanted to grab him by his shoulders and shake him until his eyes snapped back into the present moment. "Did you just want to fly? Why did you crash my car?"

"I have my reasons," he said.

"Okay," she said. She waited for him to spell them out. When it became clear that no explanation was forthcoming, she said, "I guess it's none of my business, really."

The man rolled his head and looked Lindsay straight in the eyes. "Don't pretend," he said with some effort, "that you don't know what they are."

"Excuse me?" Lindsay was quite certain she'd never seen this man before in her life. "How would I know any such thing?"

"I'm dying," he said. "At least respect that. You have to respect that."

"You gotta save your strength."

"It hurts like hell," he said, "but it's also not so bad."

"Step back," she heard an authoritative voice say, and Lindsay looked up to see a pair of EMTs rushing over from their ambulance. She saw the police were there too, parking their cruiser right smack in the middle of the lane the way they always do. The ambulance still had its lights on, pulsing useless red-and-white bursts into the afternoon sunshine, and the back doors were open. She hadn't even heard it pull up.

The paramedics crouched on either side of the man and began their unknowable rituals and incantations for bringing the nearly-dead back to life. They had power over life and death, so much more than she herself would ever have over much more mundane things. But they can't make that man *want* their help, Lindsay thought. They can't help him fly.

The entire time, the man's eyes never left Lindsay's, even while he struggled with the paramedics when they tried to give him an injection of something. It made Lindsay uncomfortable, the fact that she might be the last thing this man saw. She did not want that kind of responsibility. She wished to be anywhere else, and she cursed herself for putting them both in this situation.

"I have something for you," the man said to her.

"Are you speaking to me?" she said.

"In my pocket," he said. "Shirt pocket. It's for you."

"What could you possibly have for *me*?" Maybe she *did* know him from somewhere. "Do I *know* you?"

"Shirt pocket," he repeated. "It's important."

She slid her fingers into his shirt pocket. There was a folded slip of paper inside. "You mean this?"

"Wait," he said. "Not yet." Then he breathed in, a deep breath that rattled around his lungs for a few seconds like a loose penny in a dryer, and he died.

"Is he dead?" she asked one of the paramedics. But she already knew the answer.

"Oh yeah," he said. "Did you know him well?"

"I never saw him," she said, "before he ran his scooter into my car."

"I thought he knew you. You know, because of the note," and he pointed at Lindsay's hand. She had removed the note from the dead man's pocket without realizing it.

"Oh, it's not for me," she said quickly. "It can't be for me."

Lindsay was reluctant to open it. The very idea felt like a violation, an invasion of the man's privacy. And she was more than a little wary of what the note might contain. What if it really *was* for her?

"You should read it," the paramedic said. "It seemed important to him that you read it."

"Oh, I don't know," she said. "I don't think I should." But truth be told, her curiosity had started to get the better of her. Nothing like this had ever happened to her before. And the dead man had said that he wanted her to read the note. He'd come right out and said those very words. That was true enough.

"All right," she said. "But I still don't feel great about this."

She unfolded the small sheet of heavy bond to see a single typewritten sentence centered on the page:

I BLAME MYSELF BUT ALSO YOU

There was nothing else, no signature, no name, not even any punctuation. She turned the paper over in her hands again and again, looking for anything that might jostle a memory or deliver a sudden slap of recognition in her brain. But there was nothing on it beyond those six baffling words.

"Well? What does it say?"

She re-folded the note and shoved it into her purse before anyone could see it. "Nothing," she said.

"Well let's find out who this fella was," the other paramedic said. She rolled the broken body onto its side and felt around the seat of the man's jeans. "No wallet though."

"You're sure you don't know this man, now," the first deputy sheriff said to Lindsay. His expression said he already didn't believe her.

"Look close," urged the second.

"Maybe a former paramour?" the first suggested. "Or someone you let go from a job once, and he never got over it?"

"No, nothing like that." Lindsay felt complimented that the deputy seemed to think she might have the power to fire someone at work. *Maybe someday,* she thought. She decided not to correct his error.

"It's just that it'd help us out a lot if you knew who he was," the second deputy said. "Save us a lot of time."

"I wish I could help," she said. "I really do." But all she really wanted to do was escape.

●

The man's name turned out to be Randall Rainwater, of all things. Lindsay found this out from the brief article about the accident that ran in the *Tribune* two days later. She also learned from the article that the scooter he was driving was stolen, a fact that was graciously omitted from the obituary she found a day or two later. Between the six paragraphs that comprised those two posthumous documents of Randall Rainwater's life, Lindsay was able to piece together a few things about the man. He was thirty-six years old. He had spent some time in the Air Force at some point, though the obituary was hazy on when or for how long. He had two young daughters who lived in Idaho. He had attended Leto High School but seemed to have no further schooling; it was unclear if he ever actually graduated. He worked at a garden center over in Gulfport. He was a diehard Denver Broncos fan who also loved amateur backyard wrestling and flying drones. He was a gentle soul who would do anything for the people he loved. And he apparently stole things sometimes.

Lindsay tried Google next, hoping it might fill in a few more blanks, but it was no help. He had somehow managed to leave no significant digital footprint over the last two decades or so. She gently chewed her lower lip. There were many things she still didn't know about Randall Rainwater, things she needed to know that wouldn't be in an obituary or a terse article about a car accident.

Randall's memorial service was tomorrow at 1 p.m., at the Eldridge & Hawkins funeral home, eight or ten miles up US 19. That wasn't too far. Lindsay had never fancied herself a funeral crasher, or a crasher of any sort: she had been raised with a reverence for proper etiquette that bordered on terror, and even now she could feel her late mother's gaze, equal parts abrasive and disappointed, fall across her shoulders as she considered committing what was certainly a significant breach of good manners. One simply does not intrude upon the memorial service of a person whose death one is responsible for, even if it was an accident.

But she could see no other way.

●

The parking lot of Eldridge & Hawkins Funeral Home was just about full when Lindsay arrived, and once she found a space she very nearly convinced herself not to get out of the car at all, to just turn around and go home, maybe stop at the Chick-Fil-A across the street for lunch so the drive out here wouldn't be a total waste. But in the end, her need to know this man won out. She found a seat near the back of the room, staying as far away from the open casket at the other end as she could.

Lindsay sat and listened for the better part of an hour as a trickle of Randall's family and friends stood between the casket and the poster-sized portrait of Randall biting into a deep-fried turkey leg; the background suggested to Lindsay that the picture had been taken at Disney World. *I guess he liked roller coasters too*, she thought, but as the service wore on it became clear to her that this might be the only new information she'd turn up here. Everyone else in this room had apparently known Randall for years, and the remarks were dense with inside jokes and family shorthand and names of people who couldn't be there for one reason or another. From the context, she guessed that many of them were dead too. She decided to leave.

Lindsay waited until a lean young man in a brown thrift-store suit stood up to speak his piece on the matter of Randall Rainwater's passing. She got up the same moment he did and went the other way, back into the foyer. A middle-aged woman with a harried look about her followed close behind; Lindsay did not notice her until they were both outside.

"Oh, thank goodness," the woman said. Lindsay spun around to face her and took a quick, instinctive step back. There were a couple of other mourners out there with them, smoking and talking quietly. "Thank goodness you're here." Then, without warning, she wrapped her arms around Lindsay and drew her in tight. "We didn't know if you'd make it. I know Bernard's been trying to reach you, or at least he *says* he has. Hell, we weren't even sure we had any of your right numbers anymore, it's been so long." She released her grip after ten seconds or so, opting instead to grasp Lindsay by the shoulders. "But none of that matters now," she said. "Since you're here and all."

"Here I am, all right," Lindsay said. She was certain she'd never seen this woman before in her life.

The woman's brow scrunched. "Do you not remember me?" she asked. "Stacy. Randall's cousin."

"Of course," Lindsay said. "Of course I remember."

"I know it's been a while, and I was a lot skinnier back then."

"No," Lindsay said. "Don't be silly. I'm just tired."

"Oh, I can imagine," Stacy said. "You've had a long trip."

"Listen," Lindsay said. The service seemed to be breaking up now; more people were wandering out to the parking lot. "I think there might be a misunder—"

"Oh!" Stacy nearly shouted. "I can't believe I almost forgot. I have something for you." She turned and headed into the parking lot.

"For me?" Lindsay asked. "What could you possibly have for me?" she asked, but Stacy was already rummaging through the trunk of her car.

When she returned, she carried an oversized beige shoebox with the word *CHRISTA* scrawled across the lid in green sharpie.

Christa, Lindsay suddenly realized, must be the ex-wife. The one in Idaho.

"He wanted you to have this," Stacy said. She held the box out to Lindsay.

"What's in it?" she asked.

Stacy shrugged. "I don't look in boxes that ain't addressed to me. Could be a box full of all the love letters he never sent you. Or it could be all the bills he ain't been paying. Hell, might just be receipts and gum wrappers."

The box felt substantial but not heavy in Lindsay's hands. She fought the urge to rush over to her car, rip the lid off the box, and root through whatever was inside. She could not believe her luck—*this is a gold mine, is what this is, a gift from the Lord*—and for a moment even forgot that she wasn't the person Stacy thought she was.

"Thank you for this," she said.

"Oh of course, dear," Stacy said. "I imagine you're probably still reeling and whatnot from all this."

"Yes," Lindsay said. "I reckon I'm still a little shell-shocked."

"Do you know how to get to the cemetery?" Stacy asked. "You can ride with me if you want."

Lindsay gestured toward her car. "Thank you, but I drove here, so it'd probably be easier if—"

"Oh, goodness," Stacy said. "What *happened* to your *car*?" It took Lindsay a moment to realize she was referring to the dent in the hood.

"The neighbor's kid backed a U-Haul into it a couple weeks back."

Stacy stopped. "Wait, did you *drive* here?"

"Well, sure, I guess."

"All the way from Idaho?"

Lindsay quickly realized her mistake and scrambled to cover it; of course she'd *flown*, of course she had, naturally the car was a rental, because who would be silly enough to waste all that time driving? But before she could get all the words out, they were joined by a bald, pear-shaped man in shiny mirrored aviator sunglasses. He looked to be in his late fifties at least, and he wore a beard like Spanish moss.

"Who you got there?" the man asked Stacy.

"It's Christa, of course," she said. "She drove all the way from Boise to be here."

"Christa," the man repeated.

"Randall's wife?" Stacy said. "You *must* remember her."

The man looked at Lindsay from behind those reflective lenses. "I don't know *who* that is," he said, jabbing his index finger toward her. "But it ain't Christa."

"I'm so sorry," Lindsay said, twisting her torso to protect the shoebox in case Stacy made a move to retrieve it. She watched the expression on Stacy's face shift from bafflement to shocked comprehension to disgust. "There's been a huge misunderstanding here. I'm sorry. I'll just—yeah, I'll just go."

She turned and walked quickly over to her car, a few spaces away.

"Hey," Stacy called. "Just a minute, now."

"I'm sorry," Lindsay yelled. Some of the other mourners turned their heads to see what the commotion was about. "You'll never see me again, I promise."

"Come back here," Stacy said. Lindsay heard the rapid clicking of her heels in pursuit. "You bring that back. That box is not *for* you."

"I'm calling the police," the man with the sunglasses said in a voice that sounded intentionally too loud. But by then Lindsay was in her car, fumbling for her keys, the box wedged under her seat for safekeeping. She heard a sharp tapping at the passenger's-side window and she jumped; she wasn't sure but she may have even let out a little yelp. It was Stacy, rapping at the glass with a quarter.

"You come on out of there and talk to me," she said.

But instead Lindsay jammed the key into the ignition and twisted it. The engine spat once or twice before catching, and she stepped on the gas and turned away from the crowd of mourners, toward the way out. In her rearview, she saw the man with the sunglasses holding his phone up, probably taking a picture of her license plate.

"I'm sorry!" she yelled again as she merged into traffic, but her windows were up and no one could hear her.

Lindsay did not stop at the Chick-Fil-A across the street from Eldridge & Hawkins. Instead, she drove to Suncoast Body Shop on 38th Avenue to get an estimate on the damage to the front end of her Jetta. She'd meant to do that all week but just hadn't got around to it. In the wake of her humiliating experience at the funeral home, it suddenly became her most important priority, as if fixing the dent right *now* would somehow let her take back what had just happened.

On her way to the body shop, she pulled into a parking lot in front of a lonely glass-and-concrete office building. It was at least three football fields away from its nearest neighbor and there were no trees, only a fountain in front and a kidney-shaped retention pond on one side. She drove to the far end of the parking lot, near the pond and away from the other cars, and parked. The shoebox rested on the passenger's seat; her hand rested on the lid.

I should take it back, she thought. *I don't have a right to know this man, not like this. Certainly, the service is over by now; I could take the box back and just leave it by the door.* The funeral home people would probably figure it out and then they could call Stacy to come get it.

She visualized setting the box down in front of the door, square in the middle of the chewed-up mat, and in her mind she heard the door open just as she was bent all the way over and she looked up to see the funeral director and Stacy and the bearded man with the sunglasses, all looking down on her and scowling. Her chest drew tight and she took a deep breath. *No,* she decided. *I won't be going back there.*

Randall had wanted the box to go to Christa. But Christa had not cared enough to come and get it. Christa had not been there to receive Randall's last accusing words, like some sort of inverted last rites. To comfort him as the life receded out from his body. To hear him take that horrible last breath—what did they call that? Oh yes. A death rattle—and carry that sound around with her for the rest of her life.

She hadn't even been there to watch them put him in the ground. The father of her daughters. Lindsay could barely even imagine such a spiteful thing.

The box may have had Christa's name on it, but Lindsay was its rightful owner. She had *earned* it, in a way that Christa had not. She had earned the right to know who Randall Rainwater was after all.

Lindsay took the box onto her lap and removed the lid.

●

"The *hell* did you hit, lady?" the mechanic asked. He was an older man in dark blue coveralls and a Champion Auto Parts cap. The faded tattoos on his forearms were streaked with grease, and he smelled like peppermint. He squinted at the deep dent in her hood. "Deer?"

"No," Lindsay said. She was distracted, thinking about that moment—not even an hour ago—when she flipped aside the box's lid and saw just what Randall Rainwater had gone to so much trouble to earmark for his estranged wife in the event of his death. Dozens of notes, possibly more than a hundred, all typed out on that same heavy bond paper and folded once, each of them—the ones she read, anyway—just as cryptic as the one he'd insisted she take from his shirt pocket:

```
I AM NOWHERE AND NO ONE AND YOU ARE
RIGHT HERE WITH ME
IT IS TIME TO START TIME OVER
WHO CAN EXPLAIN THE TIDES
THE CIRCLE SITS INSIDE THE SQUARE
INSIDE THE CIRCLE
SASQUATCH IS REAL
```

Lindsay had pulled out note after note, opening each with a snap of her wrist until she wanted to cry. They were *all* like that, like bumper stickers for lunatics.

The mechanic nodded.

"Musta been something big, though," he said. "Dent that size. Wasn't a panther, I hope. You know they're endangered."

"*I* didn't hit anything," she said, trying to pull her mind into the present and away from thoughts of the box, the stupid box that had had no answers to give her. Only more questions. Were they poetry? Did he carry a different one in his pocket each day? Did he hand them out to people or did he recycle them? Why would he bother?

She would never know. And suddenly, she didn't care. Randall Rainwater was clearly a crazy person, and she had enough crazy people that she couldn't seem to get rid of in her life, thank you so very much.

"Don't worry," the mechanic said, laughing. "I won't tell your husband."

"My husband just died," she blurted. "My husband Randall."

The mechanic's eyes widened, and he stopped laughing. Lindsay watched his face go ash gray for a couple seconds, then flush crimson. "Aw, shit. I'm sorry. I, I didn't know. I certainly didn't mean anything by it."

Lindsay immediately wished she could take it back. She certainly hadn't meant to claim Randall as her husband; not even sixty seconds earlier she'd decided to put the man out of her mind for good. But now that she *had* claimed him—and for the second time that day—she decided to lean into it.

"What you're fixing," she said, "what I'm *paying* you to fix, that's from the accident that killed him."

The mechanic opened his mouth and turned his palms outward toward Lindsay. She waited for him to say something, but all he seemed able to do was slowly shake his head back and forth while emitting a strange stuttering throat-clearing noise.

"All he ever did for me was make my life harder anyway," she said.

"I'm so sorry," he stammered. She waved him off.

"All I need from you right now is a number," she said.

His estimate was $3800, give or take.

"I wish I could do better for you, on account of your loss and all," he said, looking at the floor. "I can throw in a loaner for free, if that helps. But that's as far as I can go."

"Fine," she said, even though she was pretty sure the mechanic was overcharging her and her insurance would only cover twenty-five hundred, tops. *I hope you're laughing it up in hell, you asshole,* she thought, and this time she did not feel guilty.

●

Early that evening Lindsay drove the loaner out to the middle of the Sunshine Skyway Bridge, just before the hump. She parked it in the breakdown lane, switched on her hazard lights, and sat for a minute while she let her thoughts peel themselves away, one by one, until she could think clearly.

Randall was not her husband. She did not know the man. But she had claimed him twice that day, and she had killed him just last week.

When her mind was calm and she was ready, Lindsay slid over to the passenger's side and opened the door, pushing back against a gust of wind that set the bridge's thick cables to trembling.

A car barreled past, its horn blaring and then receding into a lower register, and then into nothingness. Lindsay heard a phone ringing somewhere. It wasn't until after the fourth or fifth ring that she thought to wonder where it was coming from.

The phone was about ten yards away to her right, in a small blue box on a stanchion coming out of the three-foot concrete lip that was the only thing between her and a very long drop. There was a flashing blue light on top of the box. Carefully, Lindsay made her way over to it.

"Hello?" she said.

"Hello?" a voice said. Lindsay had to strain to hear it over the wind.

"Hello again," Lindsay said. "To whom am I speaking, please?"

"Hi. I'm Bret," the voice said. It sounded like a woman's voice, but the wind made it hard to be certain. "What's your name?"

"Lindsay."

"Hi, Lindsay. It's nice to meet you," Bret said. "I work for emergency services. I wanted to make sure you were okay."

"I'm fine," she said. "How did you know I was here?"

"There are cameras running the entire length of the bridge," Bret said, and Lindsay could see them now, atop their poles fifteen feet above traffic. She had never noticed them before. "Is there anything you need to talk about? I can just listen if that's what you need."

"No, I'm good," Lindsay said. "Thanks, though."

"So you're not supposed to stop on the bridge except in case of emergency," Bret said. "Don't worry, you're not in trouble, I promise. But do you mind if I ask what made you decide to stop?"

"Somebody asked me to do something for them."

"What did they ask you to do?"

"He wanted to fly," she said. "So I'm giving him the next best thing."

"People can't fly," Bret said. "You'll just fall. It's a long way down, and that water is a lot harder than it looks."

Lindsay craned her neck to get a better look over the side.

"It is that," she said into the phone.

"Almost two hundred feet. Whatever is wrong in your life, it's not worth this," Bret said. "Even if you think it's all your fault."

She closed her eyes and saw Randall, sprawled out on the pavement, handing her his note just before he cackled and died.

"He said he blames me," Lindsay said. "That's why I'm trying to make it right."

"Do you want me to send someone?" Bret asked.

"No, thank you," Lindsay said. "If it's all the same to you, I think I am gonna hang up and drive home now."

"That's a good idea," Bret said. "I'll be keeping an eye out for you."

"Goodbye," Lindsay said, and she hung up.

Lindsay made her way back to the car, keeping her hand on the concrete lip the whole way. When she got there, she opened the passenger door and retrieved the shoebox. She took a step toward the edge; as she drew closer, the magnitude of the drop solidified in her mind. She pulled back, pushing herself against the car door.

Goddammit. This was no time for weakness. She took a breath and held it, slid one foot along the pavement until her toe touched the concrete barrier, then did the same with the other.

She realized her eyes were closed. Her eyes could not be closed for this. She needed to see it. She let out the breath she was still holding, forced her eyes open and, in a single fluid motion, raised the shoebox above her head and ripped off the lid.

Now's your chance, she thought, and just then a sharp gust took Randall's strange little notes, snatching them all out of the box and spitting them into a steep updraft, one after another until the box was empty. They went swirling and soaring high above for a few glorious seconds before the wind died again, and Lindsay watched them open and flutter and float and circle down toward the water like tired and delicate birds.

The Insomniac Traveler's Guide
to the Lost Pyramids
of Quartzsite, Arizona

The thing is—and this will come as a disappointment for you, but it wouldn't be sporting to leave you in suspense—there are no pyramids in Quartzsite, Arizona. Forget what the bartender told you. They don't exist. And neither do the camels, though this will not come as such a blow. You have seen camels before. Truth be told, you find camels to be a little off-putting.

So. No pyramids and no camels, despite both what you've been told and the implications of the town's "welcome" sign, situated just off the Interstate directly in front of the Burger King. It is about five feet high by seven feet wide and is the color of copper and sand. Arizona colors. Desert colors, which you are sick to death of by now. Beneath the town name is a simple diorama, a pyramid ringed by camel silhouettes cut from bronze sheeting.

Implications, hell. This is an outright lie, is what this is.

But you don't know any of this yet. All you have is what the bartender said, back at the HoJo in Beaumont, Texas. And the weird little guidebook she gave you.

She was young and pretty—blonde, fair-skinned, just your type—with a cagey sort of half-smile, like she knew something you didn't and wanted you to be aware of that fact. The top edge of a back tattoo poked out above her collar, but you couldn't make out what it was. She checked your ID and was nice to you when she found out you're from the same place as her mother, even after you explained that the city listed on your driver's license isn't actually your hometown. It's really just the place I left most recently, you told her. Mom never stayed in one place long enough for any of them to feel like home, probably because habitual check kiting isn't really compatible with long-term domestic stability.

She mixed you the best Manhattan you'd had in a long time. Then she mixed you another. It did not take much effort to convince her to come up to your room after her shift. But you did not get much out of the encounter; you were far too tired to feel anything.

This, of course, did not surprise you. It had already been that way for you for some time.

After, she balled herself up beside you and quickly slipped into a quiet little stream-of-consciousness monologue. You had a hard time following her at first; her narrative was slippery and elusive, and you couldn't quite focus on it. But it didn't take long for you to pick up the thread. It was the story of her own hometown, a place named Quartzsite, Arizona, and the pyramids in the desert just outside of town there. When she was a girl, she used to sneak away from her mother's trailer and go play among them in the middle of the night, alone except for the tarantulas and scorpions and rattlers and the camels, which she occasionally would climb atop and ride around. They—the pyramids, of course, not the camels—are two hundred feet high and were built thousands of years ago, by a long-lost tribe of indigenous Americans who predated the Puebloans and who had mastered astronomy and geography and even the basics of plate tectonics, centuries before any white man ever thought of such things. Then they disappeared without leaving so much as one single solitary archaeological trace of their existence.

Other than the pyramids, that is.

While she slept, you sat in bed, in that liminal state of half-wakefulness that defines your existence these days. Your mind fixated on the pyramids. Kings lived in pyramids, didn't they? Egyptian kings. Pharaohs. One thing you know about the ancient pharaohs is, when they could not sleep, they drank a psychoactive concoction made from wild lettuce stems. This is a random fact you have picked up in your research. The drink was thick and milky and contained a natural sedative—you can't remember the name of it right now, but the people at the Whole Foods back home had never heard of it. They wouldn't even try to help you. They were obviously embarrassed by their lack of knowledge, which is understandable, but a lifetime ban was, without question, an overreaction on their part.

Maybe I can do that, you thought. Forget about California altogether. Just stake your claim to a pyramid and live like a king in the Arizona desert.

In the morning, she pressed a strange little guidebook into your hands. The cover read *The Intrepid*

Traveler's Guide to the Lost Pyramids of Quartzsite, Arizona. It's only about sixty pages or so and has a vaguely amateurish look to it: the typeface isn't quite right, and the cover photo is a picture of the Grand Canyon for some reason.

I think you can use this, she said. Just don't read it until you get there. It won't make any sense before then.

Now that you are actually in Quartzsite, you flip through the book, looking for a map, coordinates, anything like that. Naturally there is no map, and your mind is too fuzzed to focus on the words long enough to parse them properly. You toss the book back onto the passenger's seat and hoist yourself up on top of your car, so you can better scan the desiccated landscape around you: the town of Quartzsite is in front of you, to the north, little more than a cluster of low-profile boxes painted to blend into the terrain. You cup your hand over your eyes and squint real damn hard, but alas, no pyramid tips poking over any of the buildings.

You check your phone, but it is no help: to be in Quartzsite is to be out of range.

So you hop down and climb back into your seven-year-old Ford Escape and drive toward those buildings, and for a while you just tool around, making last-second turns at random intervals because the town is only so big; the pyramids *must* be nearby somewhere.

But you don't find them. They aren't behind the self-storage place or the liquor store or the gun store. They aren't over by the library. They aren't wedged into that empty lot between the equipment rental place and the tire yard.

Suddenly the energy just drains from you, and you have to pull over. You feel weak, dizzy, shaky. Is it the insomnia? Low blood sugar? The late afternoon desert sun? Could be any or all of those, really. You haven't eaten since Las Cruces, and you haven't really slept in . . . well, let's just say it's been a while.

You wonder, and not for the first time, if you can actually die from insomnia. Your doctor said no, it's not possible. It's certainly not *good* for you, he added, and then he started freestyling on all the ways insomnia can fuck you up good: weight gain, loss of cognition, high blood pressure, early-onset dementia, diabetes, memory loss, depression, projectile incontinence—but no no, he reassured you, it can't *kill* you.

The internet says different, though.

There is an article on a semi-reputable but well-known news site about a man who died after going without sleep for eleven days. This, of course, is actually a bit less than the world's record for consecutive hours spent awake, the provenance of said record being somewhat murky, thanks to the major record-keeping bureaus' reluctance to encourage such behavior in pursuit of fame, or at least notoriety and endorsement deals.

On Wikipedia you found the story of an Egyptian man who died after not sleeping for seven months. Seven *months*. His brain slowly atrophied until it withered into something resembling a dried-out peach. Wikipedia actually describes his condition as "fatal insomnia." *Fatal.* The word's right there in the name, so clearly your doctor doesn't know what he's talking about.

But that's par for the course with him anyway. He always tells you you're fine, or how it's all in your head, or how you really need to stop reading WebMD. Which is, of course, easy for him to say. He's not the one suffering, is he?

Still, you're probably in the clear, more or less. Technically, you are rarely awake for more than thirty hours at a time; usually your body will simply go into standby mode for an hour, possibly two, so you are getting *some* sleep. But it's always that fragile, surface-level sleep, and never for longer than a couple hours, never more than just enough to tease you with a cruel reminder of what you're missing.

So it probably won't kill you. But you never really know, do you?

Just then you notice a small sign by the side of the road that reads *Ham Fest—this way!* Your stomach rumbles. A nice ham sandwich sounds like just the thing.

After a few minutes of driving around, you find the Ham Fest at the local Expo Hall, which is little more than an oversized garage at the far end of the town's main drag. The parking lot is crammed full of RVs and campers. The event itself turns out to be something other than what you expected. There are no smokers. No honey glaze. No sandwiches. It is instead a convention of ham radio operators, a motley collection of random neckbeards and jittery survivalists engaging in a hobby whose continued existence in the age of the internet makes no sense at all.

Some people are just committed to doing things the hard way. It's a common enough point of pride for certain personality types.

But they seem friendly enough as you amble from booth to booth. Or at least, not overtly hostile, which is good enough. You wonder if it's because you look like you're one of them.

You really hope that's not it.

Hey, you say to an overweight man at one of the booths. He sits in a cheap folding lawn chair, from which he has greeted everyone who has passed by in the two minutes you've been watching him.

Hey yourself, he says. How can I help you?

You know much about this town?

Well I would hope so, he says. I haven't missed a Ham Fest in fourteen years.

You know about the pyramids?

Pardon me? he asks. Pyramids? What pyramids you mean?

The ones here in Quartzsite, you say. They're out by a trailer park somewhere, I think. But I can't find 'em.

I'm sorry, he says. I'm afraid I don't get the joke.

Forget it, you say, and you turn to walk away.

Then you remember: the guidebook. Here, you say. I can show you. And you hand him the book. He takes it from you and leafs through the pages.

What the hell is this supposed to be? he asks you.

Exactly what it says, you say. He shakes his head.

Ronnie! he yells out. In a booth across the concourse, a short, lean man with a shaved head turns, eyebrows raised. The fat man waves him over. You ever seen this before? he asks Ronnie, and gives him the book. Ronnie's a local, the man explains.

Wow, where'd you get *this*? Ronnie asks.

You've seen it before? you ask.

Not for a long ass time. There was some woman printed up a bunch of these back in the day. Used to hand 'em out in the parking lot at the Sav-Mor. Nobody really knew why. She was probably touched in the head or something.

Sounds like too much peyote, the fat guy says.

Yeah, maybe, Ronnie says with a laugh. Sounds about right.

You remember her name? you ask him. Where she lived?

She had a trailer out in the desert, he says. Don't remember her name. She was mostly just a low-grade nutcase until the state came and took her kid away, I remember that.

So there's no pyramids then.

No, there's no pyramids. Shit, man, you *read* any of this thing?

A little, you say.

Okay then, Ronnie says, and he hands you back the book.

Okay, you say. Thanks anyway.

Back in the car, you realize you still have not eaten all day. Thwarted in your quest for ham, you contemplate returning to the Burger King.

There is no shame in that. It is a perfectly serviceable Burger King. Try the chicken sandwich.

●

You actually tried reading the guidebook two nights ago, after you ran out of gas on the western edge of Texas hill country, which is to say the middle of fucking nowhere. The upside to that little miscalculation—you thought you had enough gas to make Fort Stockton with ease, but you didn't factor the hills into that equation—was the gift of a suddenly abbreviated driving day, like that time when Kenny, out of the blue, just gave you the afternoon off for no reason. Clocking out early is always nice. The downside, of course, was spending the night in your car—no phone reception out there either—by the side of the road, and the strong possibility of dying before sunrise, most likely falling victim to a coyote or psycho hitchhiker. Or a psycho hitchhiker with a pet coyote. At the very least, you'd probably die of exposure, whatever *that* is.

Gave you the afternoon off. That's not bad. You always have had a way with euphemism.

After two hours only a handful of cars had passed. None of them stopped.

Might be here a while.

Maybe you could read a book to kill the time.

She said you should wait, though. Said it wouldn't make any sense until you get to Quartzsite.

But books don't really work that way, do they? They either make sense or they don't.

You opened it to a random page. It was dense with text, two columns full of old typewriter font running the length of each facing page, scarcely a paragraph break to be found. The next page was exactly the same, as were most of the rest. It looked nothing like the Lonely Planet guides you're used to, that's for sure.

You squinted at the page and tried to follow along, but the light was fading and there was so little space between the lines and you just couldn't hold the words in your head for more than a few seconds, you were so tired. A few random phrases popped out at you: *Shadows of the equinox . . . tertiary binary subduction wave . . . interdimensional trans-subsidence portal . . .*

You gave up and tossed it back onto the passenger's seat. Guess she was right.

Or maybe Ronnie was right. None of this book makes any goddamn sense. It's either complete gibberish or science far too deep for you to grasp.

But even if you don't understand what it *says*, you do understand what it *is*.

This is a test.

She meant for you to have those pyramids because they will let you sleep.

But you have to *find* them first.

So tonight, the sand is upon you, in your hair, your shoes, your socks, the folds of your underwear, out here in the desert just west of Quartzsite, near a long-abandoned doublewide. The sand runs through your hands with each scoop cast over your shoulder and swirls around your head with every gust of wind. It works its way into your mouth and eyes. It slowly lays its claim to you, so slowly you don't notice it, so slowly you can't stop it.

On that future night when you do finally sleep for real—and that night will come, eventually—you may dream of this moment. You may wonder how you escaped the creeping sands; you will have no memory of it. Over time, the lines between dream and memory will blur, and eventually you will start to think of this night, this night right now, the night you tried to unearth the lost pyramids of Quartzsite with your own bare hands, as the former.

It's not, though.

You are here. You are working. Any minute now, you expect to feel your knuckles knock against something hard, just below the surface of the sand.

Any minute now.

Maybe it will glint in the moonlight.

Maybe it will be made of silver.

You've got all night to find out.

Tube Man

The epiphany that enabled Carl to finally tube-size his life came, as those things often do, one Wednesday night over a plate of mushroom-and-bacon risotto. It was so powerful that it compelled him to slam down his fork and shove himself away from the heavy teak dining table without realizing he was doing it.

"Are you okay?" Sara said. "You've been acting weird."

Of course, he thought. *Of course of course of course.*

"I'm fine," he rasped. "Never better." And it was true, though it was also true that he had been acting strangely in recent weeks. Or, at least, differently.

Sara set her wine glass down, folded her arms and appraised him. "I don't believe you," she said, drumming her French tips on her bicep. "You definitely don't *sound* okay."

"It's nothing," he said. "The wine went down the wrong pipe, is all." He dug his phone out of his pocket and began poking at the display.

"Hey, you know the rules," Sara said. "No phones at the table."

"I have to look something up real quick." Normally, Carl was the stickler for enforcing the no-phones rule. It was one of his methods of shoring up the ever-sagging barrier between his working hours and his personal time. The last thing he wanted to do over dinner was respond to code reviews or pull requests or inane questions from QA or the product team or—god forbid—marketing about the new build or issues with the upcoming deploy, and he knew that if he didn't go to extreme lengths to make himself inaccessible, he'd never get even a moment's peace. Such were the travails of being the best coder in the company.

"I don't care what you're doing. The rule is the rule," she said. "It was your idea anyway."

"Fine," Carl said, and he stood up and strode into the living room. By the time he got there, he had his answer, but it would have to wait until morning.

"The biggest we got is a 55 gallon model," the man told him over the phone the next day. "What were you looking to use it for?"

"How wide is the opening?" Carl asked.

"Lemme see here . . . says twenty-three and-three-eighths."

"And they're what, three feet tall or so?"

"Not quite," the man said. "More like thirty-four-and-a-half inches. So, almost."

"Hmmmmm." That would be a tight fit, even for Carl. Still, he was sure it could be done. He had seen people putting dead bodies in large plastic drums in movies and on TV. Some of those bodies had been a lot fatter than he was. "I think I'd better get three," he said. "Can I pick them up tomorrow?"

●

Carl had been thinking about tubes for months, ever since he read an article in the Sunday travel section about how men in Tokyo live in them. Just long enough to lie down in, these tubes form a honeycomb, stacked three high, each with a built-in TV screen the size of a cereal box and a flimsy privacy curtain strung across the opening. There are entire hotels of these ultra-spartan accommodations, each floor stuffed with pods upon pods of anonymous salarymen, no room for much of anything beyond the occupant and his thoughts.

He was impressed with that kind of asceticism, that willingness to live without in a city where there was just so *much* of everything—people, food, bacteria, stimuli, perversion. No, more than just impressed. *Fixated* was more like it. Lately he could think of little else.

"It's not because they don't *want* any more space," Sara pointed out one night over a glass of viognier on the back patio. "They're stockbrokers or whatever, not monks. They want space, believe me. They just can't afford it. Everyone knows Tokyo is crazy expensive. It's the most expensive city in the world."

"Not this year," Carl said. He tried to tune out the frantic buzzing of the cicadas, that indigenous dinner music of summertime, but could not. He scowled. The very sound of it made him sweat. "Forbes says it's Hong Kong."

"Same difference. Anyway, the point is, if they could get a decent two-bedroom in a rent-controlled building, they'd be all over it. Especially if there's a washer-dryer hookup." Which is exactly what the article had said, but for Carl, that was beside the point. His whole life, he had carried around a mental inventory of appliances and gadgets that, taken together, set out the implicit baseline requirements of civilized life. A car. An iPod, or before that, a Walkman. Cable TV with 300 high-definition premium channels. A microwave oven. A tablet.

But the tube men, they needed none of those things. They needed nothing, and because of that, they had everything.

Carl had plenty of things. More things than he could count. He was *drowning* in things, and for what? Did they make him any smarter, or more virile, or even happier? For the most part, no. He was tired of needing them, and had been for a long time. He just hadn't known it until he read that article.

Sara, on the other hand, liked things just fine.

"I think the microwave is broken," she told him the next afternoon. She fiddled with the power cord and poked at the front panel's inert buttons. No happy little electronic chirps came in response this time, as they always had before. Her fingertips tapped out an impatient staccato pattern against the granite countertop.

"Perfect," Carl said. "Let's not get a new one."

"Don't be ridiculous," she said, squinting at him. "They're like eighty bucks at Best Buy."

"I'm serious," he said.

"Whatever." She let the cord drop onto the counter. "I have to water the plants."

Carl didn't move from his chair, didn't shift his gaze from his laptop as she left. He had no intention of going to Best Buy that day, or the next, or the next. Instead, he started cooking slow dinners over the gas flame of the stovetop, or grilling meats in his oversized ceramic barbecue cooker on the patio. He reheated leftovers the same way. He made popcorn in a cavernous, heavy pot with some canola oil. And he knew that soon he would discover that he had no real need for a microwave. He never did, really, and probably never would again.

"You see?" he said to her one day, weeks later, as he warmed up some leftover barbecued chicken thighs on the stove. "No cold spots in the center. Who needs a microwave?"

"It takes so *long* though," she said. "And everything always comes out burnt."

"It's just a matter of adjusting. You'll get the hang of it."

"I don't *want* to get the hang of it. What I *want* is a microwave. I haven't lived without a microwave since I was a teenager."

Sara had spent her formative years following her mother and brother from one vaguely grubby apartment complex to the next, crisscrossing the county's less-upwardly-mobile suburbs just steps ahead of a parade of bill collectors. No fancy microwaves in *those* shitholes, that was for sure. *From humble beginnings come great things* was something her mother used to say whenever they complained about the relative hardship of their lives compared to those of their friends; they would roll their eyes whenever she said it. But now Sara thought of herself as living proof of the aphorism's inherent truth: over the years, she'd worked her way up to a comfortable position in the accounts payable department of the county's largest hospital, which is further than she'd ever really expected to get. "You know where I came from. I'm not going back to that, to having nothing. I'm civilized now and I mean to stay that way."

"Oh, just relax," he said. "We're still alive, still civilized. The only difference is we can't melt a brick of frozen lasagna in the time it takes to walk out to the mailbox and back." He smiled as he said this. He did not consider it to be any sort of deprivation.

Maybe that's how it starts, he thought. Maybe it's a matter of shedding the easy stuff first. Leaving the low-hanging fruit on the branches. Just start passively, and work up to discarding the perfectly good yet still nonessential.

Once you realize how unnecessary a thing really is, he realized, not having it is no longer a sacrifice.

Maybe that's how the tube men did it.

The next week, on Thursday, Sara came home from work carrying an unboxed forty-two-inch LCD television. She nearly tripped over the power cord dangling in front of her feet before she could set the TV on the dining room table, where Carl was working.

"Careful," he said. "You'll nick the wood. I don't want to have to refinish this table again."

"Why was this by the garbage?" she asked him. "Is it broken? You know we can't just dump this stuff in with the regular trash. It has to go to the hazardous waste place."

"It's not broken," he said.

"Then why was it out there?"

"We don't need it."

"Okay," she said. "I'm going to go plug this back in. You just leave it where it is from now on, understand?"

Carl left the TV alone after that. But on Wednesday morning of the following week, he drove his navy blue Volvo to the SouthPointe Towne Centre, a crumbling shopping mall in a faceless suburb about fifteen miles north of his house. He parked it in the asphalt savanna in front of the JCPenney before stopping in at the food court in the center of the mall, where he bought a jumbo chocolate chip cookie and a large Dr. Pepper at the Classic Cookie.

"That's a jumbo?" he asked the teenager behind the counter. The kid shrugged.

Carl took a bite from his cookie—it had been in the oven just a little too long, he could tell—and went outside to wait for the next bus. The only other people waiting were a couple of pallid, cigarette-smoking teenagers who glared at Carl when he noticed them. The number six bus picked him up about forty minutes later and, after taking him on a rambling path through countless acres of 1970s-vintage tract housing, dropped him off more than two miles from his house. All told, it took him almost three hours to get home.

"Where's your car?" Sara asked him when she got home. She plopped her cavernous purse on the table and began digging through it. "Did you have to take it in? I keep telling you we should get you something else. Volvos are overrated anyway."

"I think it was stolen," he mumbled. She stopped what she was doing and looked up.

"Stolen? You *think*?" She waited for a response. "What does that mean, you think? When's the last time you saw it? Did you call the police?"

"I haven't seen it since this morning," he said. "And I was going to file a report but I got busy with work."

"Okay," she said. "I'm going to call them now."

The police called Sara back the next day to tell her the car had been found.

"That was fast," she said.

"It was parked illegally," the officer told her. "That's how we spotted it so quick. Also, you shouldn't leave the keys inside like that. That's just asking for trouble. So when can you come and get it? We start charging for storage after three days."

"You left the car at the mall?" she asked Carl. "How did you get home?"

"I don't know what you're talking about," he said.

"You tricked me into filing a false police report," she said. "That's a crime, you know. That car wasn't stolen at all, was it? What, were you trying to collect the insurance or something?"

"I don't know what you're talking about," he said again, then looked up from his computer. Sara was watching him, her mouth drawn in a tight line, her eyes sharp. "But even if I did, so what? I hate cars. I hate having to drive anytime I want to go somewhere. I hate that cars are, are, are some kind of, like, an unofficial requirement for meaningful participation in society."

"What does that have to do with anything?" Sara asked. But he didn't hear her.

"I mean, look at what mandatory car ownership has done to the American landscape." He felt his face going purple already, but he kept going. "It's turned countless acres of open and productive farmlands and pastures into ugly, wasteful sprawl. The car, man, it's killing us as a society. Killing us. We're, we're, we're all choking to death on exhaust fumes here."

"I see," she said. "So to fix all that, you decided to trick me into filing a false police report."

Carl took a slow breath to give his tongue the second or two it needed to catch up with his brain. "There is nothing, *nothing* in my life I would rather jettison than that car."

And he had almost pulled it off. He had been so close.

"Then just sell it, for Christ's sake," she said. "And be done with it."

Maybe I will, he thought. But he hated selling things almost as much as he hated cars. It just felt more natural to abandon it instead.

A few days later, Carl went out for a run in the afternoon. Running was a new thing for him, but he was already certain it was exactly what he'd been looking for. It required no gym membership, no equipment, no special clothing. Just legs and lungs and shoes, and he already had all of those things. They would all fit in the tube with him, once he finally got to live in one. That thought, of life in a tube, a future life of simplicity and zen, kept him going as he ran, until his knees ached and his lungs itched and burned, and then he kept on going, his body screaming at him to stop, please god just stop already, until he had no choice but to obey. Then he walked home and let himself in through the back door.

He might not have even noticed the brand new microwave oven, all glass and polished chrome and hogging most of the available space on his kitchen counter, except he tripped over the cardboard box it came in. The box sat in the middle of the kitchen floor, its top flaps hanging open and looking exhausted and limp, as if it had just given birth and expelled its progeny with enough force to launch it all the way up onto to the counter.

"What the hell is this?" he asked the empty room.

Carl ran a finger along the top of the microwave, as if he couldn't quite believe it was really there. The plastic film from the factory was still stuck to the window on its door. Sitting there wedged between the bread machine and the espresso maker, the damn thing looked very much at home in its spot—almost smug, even. Carl was sure it was mocking him.

"Did you say something?" Sara appeared in the doorway.

He pointed at the microwave. "What the hell, Sara?"

She sighed, folded her arms, and leaned against the doorjamb. Her mind flashed back to a dozen or so years ago, when they first met at the hospital: she was a newly minted community college dropout with no real qualifications to speak of, while he was a lean, intense young database administrator who radiated professionalism and a kind of sexual vitality she was completely unfamiliar with. A smoldering stud with a promising future—oh yeah, she noticed him right away. But she had never been sure what he'd seen in *her* back then: she'd had no career trajectory of her own, no stability to offer in return. They had loved each other ever since, in their own peculiar way, but in this moment, looking at him standing there all petulant and sweaty and small, she wondered if maybe she hadn't actually gotten the deal she'd expected after all. "Don't you think that all . . . *this* has gone on long enough?"

"What are you talking about? No. Of course not. I'm living more with less and I like it. I love it."

"Well I don't," she said. "I'm sick of having to spend half an hour heating up leftovers. I'm sick of not being able to cook my Lean Cuisines. I don't really understand what you're doing, but it's stupid and pointless and you are never going to live in a goddamn tube, so just give it up already."

"How could you say that to me?" He grabbed a bottle of water out of the fridge and turned to face the sink, his back to Sara, before opening it.

"When you see yourself living in this tube," she said, "am I there too? Is there any room for me?"

He took a long swallow from the bottle before answering. "I guess that would depend on the size of the tube," he said. "And how much stuff you wanted to bring. But it's possible, I guess. Maybe. I don't know."

She shook her head. "What kind of an answer is that?"

It was an answer he'd been working on for some time, and he still didn't have it right, he knew that, even though he'd been anticipating the question ever since he'd first read that article about the tubes. Just in case he ever actually got the chance to live in one for real. But the things that weighed him down—the television, the car—

kept finding their way back to him. It was almost as if he *couldn't* get rid of anything, like the universe wouldn't let him shed the ballast it had fastened to him.

He felt guilty about this conversation for the rest of the afternoon, so he decided he would surprise Sara with her favorite dinner: mushroom-and-bacon risotto.

●

The next day, Carl picked up the barrels and brought them home. He cut the bottoms off all three, duct-taped the ends together and laid them all out on the living room floor, directly beneath the television he'd tried to throw away the other week. There it was. His very own tube, the bright yellow plastic almost glowing in the sunlight from the picture window. There was no privacy curtain, no tiny television screen. But the amenities would come. Or maybe they wouldn't. He hadn't decided yet. First he had to figure out how much it could hold.

He opened the hall closet, pulled out a goose-down comforter, shoved it into the tube and tamped it down around the bottom. Then he grabbed his favorite pillow and climbed in. His shoulders cleared the tube with a few inches to spare, and he had plenty of extra room at both ends. But he didn't have much room on either side, or in front of his face. He could barely lift his arms from his sides. His breathing quickened; wait, was he claustrophobic? Are you fucking *kidding?* No. No, no. Calm down, he thought. This is fine. The synthetic aroma of the probably carcinogenic plastic was almost overpowering. He felt himself getting dizzy. Do not puke in this thing, he warned himself. If he did, he knew he'd never be able to climb inside it again. He'd have to air it out before he moved in here for good; just get a fan, put it at one end and let it blow for an hour or two. And his back—that was going to be a problem too. It was already starting to strain because he couldn't lay flat, thanks to the curvature of the tube itself. A good engineer should have thought of that, he chided himself.

He forced himself to lie still in that tube for two solid minutes. After thirty seconds or so, his breathing began to even out again. This could work. It *could*.

He'd need more than bedding to live in a tube. He was afraid to even try to sleep without his CPAP machine, even though his doctor had told him several times that his apnea wasn't all that severe. And he couldn't sleep without his white noise machine even if he wanted to, because he needed something to drown out the sound of his own breathing. The air whistling through his nostrils could keep him awake for hours. So those things were must-keeps, and he set them both down in the empty space at the top of the tube, up near his head.

What else? Books and clothes, Carl told himself. And my laptop, for work. I can get along fine without anything else. He climbed out of the tube and looked up at the overstuffed bookcase on the other side of the room. Books—his books, mostly—spilled out of it.

He pulled one book—*Programming in Python*—from the shelf. Did he need this anymore? He knew Python. He used it regularly. Did he really need a reference guide that was years out of date compared to the information he could find online?

But how will people know I'm a software developer if I don't have any programming books on my shelf?

Wait. What kind of shelf space would he have in a tube? And it's not like he was planning to have guests over. *Hey, why don't you guys come on over Friday and see the tube? It's where I keep my coding library, so in case you didn't believe me when I told you that's what I did for a living, I can prove it by showing you some books.*

He stood there, cradling the book in his hands for another minute and a half before setting it on the floor. This is the keep pile, he decided. Over the next half hour, the keep pile grew larger and larger as Carl pulled title after title off the shelves. Sometimes he flipped through the pages and pretended he hadn't yet made up his mind to keep it. Others just went straight from shelf to pile, until there were more books in the keep pile than there were left in the bookcase.

I'll come back to that, he thought. Maybe focusing on clothes would be easier. All he really needed was a couple pairs of jeans, a pair of shoes, some socks and underwear, and some shirts. Maybe a jacket. Clothes would be easy.

Carl's t-shirts had all been stuffed into translucent plastic tubs—three of them, he'd bought them at the Container Store years ago—which he kept under the bed. He dragged them out, then stood back and apprised them, hands on hips. There had to be more of them in there than he could wear in a month. *How the hell did this happen?* he wondered. Hadn't he just given away a whole box of them to the Salvation Army a few months back?

He pulled the shirts out of their tubs, one at a time, and examined each one, looking for holes or frayed stitching, stretched necks or permanent stains. Anything that might give him an excuse to discard it. But he'd already given all those shirts away. Most of the ones he had left were gray or off-white and had come from one of the countless technology industry conferences he'd attended over the years. Others advertised bookstores or record stores in some faraway city. Those were mostly black. Here was one from the British Museum, a souvenir of his only trip abroad to date.

What did it all amount to? Wearable documentation of all the places he'd been. Nothing more. Do I *need* that if I remember the experience? That's enough. Isn't it?

Carl scooped up as many shirts as he could carry and hauled them into the living room, dropping them onto the keep pile. He crouched down, yanked the bedding out of the tube, and started lining the bottom with books, until they formed a nearly-even surface. He stuffed the bedding back in, spreading it across the platform of books, and climbed back inside. His face was now so close to the top of the tube that he could feel his own breath refracting off the plastic and dissipating around his face each time he exhaled.

"What the hell is this?" Sara said.

Shit, he thought. Is it 5:30 already?

"It's my tube," Carl said from inside it. "I made a tube. What do you think?"

"It's a goddamn mess is what I think," she said. He could see her form only as a shadow falling across his tube. She was an outline, a blur, a slight cosmetic blemish in the plastic. "There's stuff everywhere. What the hell, Carl?"

"I'm deciding what I can live without," he said. "I need to see it all in front of me."

"I see something I can definitely live without," she said. "This—*whatever* it is. This tube. And everything in it, Carl. Everything."

"Well as it turns out, there actually isn't any room for you in here anyway."

"Okay. Well I'm leaving, so that's just fine," she said. "I'm leaving you to your tube. I've had enough of all this bullshit. I'm going to Georgina's. Take a few days and get this . . . *thing* out of here. Take whatever else you need. But I don't want to see you or it when I come back. I've had *enough*."

"I'm not actually going to live in here, you know. Not in this one, anyway. This is just a test. A lifestyle prototype."

"Goodbye, Carl," he heard her say from the foyer. Her heels clacked across the tiled floor.

"Don't forget the microwave," he called after her, but the door slammed just as his mouth began to form the *m* sound.

He stayed in the tube after she left. He didn't know how long, but it was long enough for the light inside the tube to fade from a synthetic dandelion tint into a washed-out gray. The room was silent. Carl realized he had to pee. What did the tube men do when they had to go? The article hadn't said. Did they use adult diapers? Did they all share a communal bathroom? That seemed to Carl like a loophole, a cheat, a way to have something without taking responsibility for the fact that you want it.

The pressure on his bladder grew more insistent. He ignored it.

The room was dark now, really dark.

Carl lay there, perfectly still, his mind finally as quiet as the rest of the house. After a while he didn't feel the pressure on his bladder anymore. He snaked his arm into the empty space above his head and felt around until he found the remote control, and then the TV screen suddenly bathed the tube in its electric blue light. He couldn't see anything from inside the tube, but he didn't care. He could hear it—grating voices in a pawn shop somewhere, bickering over how much money they wanted in exchange for some of the things that had long ago come to own them—and that was enough. *This is okay,* he thought. Even the tube men get their own televisions.

Singapore Song

I t's barely 9:30 in the morning on Memorial Day and Causeway Beach is already nuts-to-butts with assorted jet-ski rednecks, sunrise drunks, and probable transients. The sun is relentless and the air is sticky and still. My father takes the turnoff in a soft sweeping arc, bringing the family station wagon—a rust-red Volaré—around much more slowly than necessary. Traffic behind us slows, stops, broods over the inconvenience. A horn or two blats somewhere in the near distance, but my father, focused on the task at hand, gives no indication of having noticed.

"Goddammit," he says. Our trailer is not cooperating. He slows the wagon to a stop, checks all the rearview mirrors from left to right, then checks them again in reverse. "I can't see around it."

My mom moves to get out. "I can guide you."

"Hold on." My father looks in the rearview at the two of us; Jack grins back while I pretend not to notice. "How about it, kiddo?"

"Me?" I look out the window at the crowd. Every last one of them is staring right at us. I sink back into my seat a little. "I don't know."

"Sure you can. Look, I get it. You're twelve now. You're embarrassed by this whole enterprise."

"I'm not." It's an obvious lie.

"Yes you are," Jack sings back at me. He is six years old and an idiot.

"Shut up, dork."

"See, even your brother can see it," my father says. "But I don't care about what people think and neither should you. That only gets in your way. You need to learn not to be so timid."

"Okay," I say. My father's philosophy of life is that growth comes from doing the things you least want to do. If you're afraid of heights, climb trees until you're comfortable perched on the highest branch. If you're afraid of the ocean, have someone throw you over the side of a boat again and again until being in the water is second nature. And if you're shy and self-conscious, the only thing for it is to embarrass yourself in front of strangers until you understand they have no power over you. "But I don't think—well, I don't know what to do."

"Just watch where the trailer's going and tell me which direction I need to turn," he says. "And let me know when to straighten out. You tell me if I'm not lined up with the ramp. Left. Right. Straight. Stop. That's only four things to remember. It could not be easier. Got that?"

I sigh. "I got it." I unbuckle the seat belt. I am certain I will regret this.

"You don't have to," my mom says. "It's all right."

"It's fine," I mutter, and I get out. Jack watches in uncharacteristic silence.

"Get on the other side where your dad can see you," my mom calls after me, and I jog around the front end of the station wagon, not because I suddenly feel any great enthusiasm for the morning's agenda, but because I know the faster we can get this tub in the water, the sooner we can go home.

"Holy shit," someone says behind me. "*Look* at that fuckin' thing." And he's right: the paint doesn't match and there are tiny globs of unsanded fiberglass here and there and you can kind of see where the plywood panels butt up to each other and the whole thing just looks . . . unfinished, somehow.

This homemade sailboat is what my father has to show for five months of unemployment. This is *all* he has to show for it: there's no new job and, according to the fragments of late-night conversations that have floated down the hallway and into my bedroom recently, not much money left in the savings account. From what I can tell, he stopped looking for work altogether two or three months ago. "Reaganomics has shit the bed but good," I overheard him say to my mother the other night, during yet another discussion about his next move: lately she has been trying to get him to go back to school, become the architect he once aspired to be, but he shoots that idea down every time. Too old for that nonsense, he says. She is the only one of us who does not see that school is not his next move. This boat is. It's the last card he has to play.

My father does not react to the continued shout-outs from the peanut gallery, and I wonder for a moment if he can hear them. But of course he can; his window is rolled all the way down.

"You ready?" my father asks me. "If I'm not lining up with the ramp, yell out which direction to turn. Got it?"

"How do I know when to straighten out?"

"You got eyes, don't you?" He shifts into reverse, gives the gas pedal a tap, and the wagon crawls backwards, pushing the trailer off to the right, toward the ramp.

●

A crowd has gathered to watch my father work. He moves about quickly in the boat, threading lines through metal rings and eyelets, raising the mast upright and fastening it into place and lashing the heavy canvas sails to it, tightening and adjusting the myriad other parts I don't know the names for. The trailer is on the ramp now, its wheels just touching the water line. My mom and Jack and I stand in a line in front of the crowd, watching silently. My father does not want our help. We will only get in his way.

"All right," he keeps saying as he makes everything ready. "All *right*." He occasionally pairs this with a *goddammit* or two.

"Everything okay in there?" my mom asks.

"It's fine," he calls out. He is hunched over and his voice is muffled.

"You sure?"

"*Yes*. It's fine. *Jeee*-zus." He continues to root around the deck, down where we cannot see him. After a few more minutes, he stands upright. He is sweating and breathing heavy; his face is flushed pink. He opens his mouth to say something but stops as he seems to notice the crowd for the first time. They are all still watching him, as if they expect him to describe what they are seeing with their own eyes, to explain himself. He claps his hands once and rubs them together.

"Welcome, one and all," he calls out, like a revival preacher. "To the float test, shakedown cruise and, with any luck, the maiden voyage of the . . . *Singapore Song*." He looks down at me and winks. "Singapore Song. Get it?"

"No," I admit. "Is it a joke?"

"I just now made it up. It's a pun."

"I don't get it."

"Never mind," he says. "Forget it." He turns back to the crowd. "I built this boat with my own two hands and all the extra time that the capriciousness of modern-day capitalism chose to suddenly bestow upon me in the form of an extended bout of unemployment, and today is the day she goes into the water for the very first time. It's a heady moment, to be sure. Almost spiritual, in its own way. So while I do appreciate your interest and your emotional support right now, I must ask that you back up and give us the room we need to do what we came here to do. Thank you so much." And he bows.

"Picked a hell of a day for a sail," someone calls out. "Got no wind."

"It'll pick up," my father says. It is less of an assurance and more of a sidelong command to the elements. "All I need is a quick spin right around here to see if she can keep the water out. If she does, I'll swing back and pick these three up, and we'll be off to South America before you can say *vaya con Doritos*."

This again. He's been saying this kind of thing a lot lately, but I can't tell if he's really serious about it. It fits with other outlandish things he's said over the years, absurdities I believed solely on the basis of his having uttered them.

"Chile's a long sail," he said to me once. "We may have to just make do with Peru. Doodily-doo!"

Another time he said, "I'm not saying we're really going to Chile. But I'm not *not* saying it either."

"Your mother would never go for it," he said once when I asked him about it directly, and his blunt, artless reply suggested this had been the real issue the whole time.

"That's right," my mom said from the other room. "I wouldn't," and there was a finality in her voice that I rarely heard from her.

I glance over at my mom now, to gauge her reaction to what he just said. Her face is unreadable.

"How's it look down there?" my father hollers down to me. "Everything all squared away?"

I have no idea what *squared away* is supposed to look like. Still, I make a big show of examining the trailer, the hull, the wheels. I try to look as serious as possible while doing it, by squinting and gently biting my bottom lip. I don't see anything that looks obviously wrong. No split seams between plywood panels, no extra nails where they shouldn't be. "Looks fine to me," I yell back.

"All right," he says. "We'll be in Chile before you know it. Diane, start 'er up and wheel me in." And he pulls his ridiculous captain's hat as far down on his head as it will go, folds his arms across his chest and tilts his face slightly skyward, looking a bit like Washington crossing the Delaware in reverse.

I watch him hold that pose as the trailer creeps backward until the water licks against the bottom of the hull. "Avast!" my father suddenly shouts. "Avast! *Stop*, for Chrissakes!" My mother slams on the brakes.

"What's wrong?" she yells from the driver's seat. My father looks over to me and, with a wave of his hand so quick I might have imagined it, invites me aboard.

"Really?" I ask.

"It's a historic moment," he says. "I think you've earned the right to see it up close. You coming or not?"

My father's modus operandi has always been to do all the important things himself, involving other people only when all that's left for them to do is gaze admiringly upon his work. An invitation to crew his boat on its float test is the last thing I expected today. I hustle up onto the trailer tongue and pull myself over the bow and into the boat before he can change his mind.

"Put your life vest on!" my mom calls to me. My father digs a ratty orange vest out of one of the storage bins and hands it to me. The straps are frayed and it smells earthy and mildewed. I put it on.

Now we are moving again. I feel the water accepting the weight of the boat as the hull frees itself from its cradle. It's floating. Holy *shit*. This is actually *working*. I remember all those days I came home from school to the toasted smell of recently-cut plywood, or the high scream of the circular saw blade doing its work, or the patient sound of the sanding block rubbing against the hull, the sour tang of paint thinner always hanging in the air. I remember my father working for months to turn a pile of wood into something more than the sum of its parts, something that could justify his jobless existence, if only to himself.

And I remember being certain that he'd fail.

My father dashes aft and fires up the tiny outboard motor, guiding us backwards and away from the ramp, out into the bay. Twenty feet. Thirty. A hundred feet. The *Singapore Song* is well and truly launched now. The rednecks crowding the ramp all hoot and clap and raise their cans of Budweiser in tribute.

●●

My father cuts the outboard once the *Singapore Song* is about a hundred yards out. He slides down in his seat and tilts his head back, turning his face toward the sun. The boat bobs like an empty soda bottle in the wake of a passing Jet Ski. Atop the mast, the flag flutters a bit, suggesting that the wind is starting to blow, just as he said it would. Is it enough to run up the sails? I have never sailed before and don't know the answer, but one thing I am certain of is that in this moment, my father is thinking of Chile.

I stand and wave to the crowd on the boat ramp. Several of them wave back, or pump their fists in the air, or let out a whoop. Somehow, our victory is their victory too. They are behind us all the way, the opposite of the neighborhood dads who hovered in the driveway and silently rooted for my father to fail. They constantly circled around the garage door like seagulls above a beach picnic, trying to figure out why a grown man with a house and a family and the standard-issue set of suburban responsibilities would spend his time, energy, and, most important, his money on building a wooden boat when there were so many already out there, just waiting for him to buy them.

I wondered the same thing. It took me a long time to work up the courage, but one day I asked him: *why are you building this thing, anyway?*

My father was silent for a long time, long enough that I thought he might not have heard me. "Because if I don't do something," he said eventually, "I will lose my fucking mind."

"I think the wind's picking up," I say.

"I told you," he says. "Just a matter of time." He doesn't move toward the halyard, though. Instead he stays like he is for a couple minutes, soaking up the sun, feeling the breeze against his face, listening to the waves lap against the hull. "We'll put the sails up in a minute." I smile. This is his moment. He earned it by himself. It's a relief to see him succeed again.

I don't notice the water pooling at my feet until it has soaked through my shoes and socks. By then it is more than half an inch deep. I see the pool bubbling gently in the center as more water gushes in.

"Dad," I say. "There's water."

"Yeah, all around us, kiddo," he says, not moving from his spot by the tiller.

"No," I say. It's easily a half-inch deeper than when I noticed it, just a few seconds ago. "In the boat."

That gets his attention. He springs up from his seat and vaults over the center bulkhead to where I sit, in the bow. "Goddammit," he says. He shoves his hands into the puddle and waves them around, like he is trying to push the water out of the way so he can get a better look at the problem. "Why didn't you say something sooner?" he snarls at me, but he does not wait for an answer. Instead, he bounds back to the outboard motor and yanks the cord until it sparks to life.

"Grab onto something up there," he shouts to me. "With any luck, maybe we can stay dry today." He guns the outboard and we shoot forward, straight at the boat ramp, and the significance of what is happening—we are sinking; *sinking!*—finally registers with me.

I cup my hand over my eyes and squint. The spectators congregate at the ramp again; they can see something's not right. My mother, standing on top of the Volaré, watches us through binoculars while Jack pesters her to look for himself. She ignores him.

Just then there is a harsh scraping sound and the boat comes to an instant shuddering stop. I slide forward and land in the pool at my feet; it's up to my ankles now. My father is nearly pitched headlong overboard, but somehow he manages to grab hold of something and stay upright and dry. Water slops over the gunwale. The *Singapore Song* is aground.

"Shit," I say.

"Yeah," my father says. His breathing is ragged. "Shit indeed."

"I think we hit the bottom."

"Congratulations on your keen mariner's instincts," he says.

"How are we gonna get back?"

"Well, we could wait for the rescue helicopters to show up, or we could swim the hundred feet or so back to shore. Your choice."

"Okay." I quickly climb up on the gunwale. I want nothing more than to get off this ruined boat and swim to shore, away from my father's scowl, away from the shattering disappointment of what should have been his triumphant moment, away from the insistent feeling that this was my fault because I found the leak. "Should I keep this vest on?"

"I'd be surprised if there's more than about four feet of water here, so you probably don't need it," he says. "But your mother's watching. So keep it on."

I hold my breath and leap as far from the boat as I can. My toe grazes the bottom as I hit the water, but the vest, awkward and constraining, quickly yanks me back up to the surface. I dog-paddle toward the ramp until the water is shallow enough for me to walk the rest of the way.

My mom rushes over to me and crouches so she can check me over for damage.

"Are you okay? I saw you took a fall out there. Did you hurt yourself?"

"I'm fine, Mom," I say, and I turn back toward the water to see my father hauling down the small American flag from the top of the mast. He rolls it up and stuffs the bundle into the back pocket of his shorts, steps up onto the bow, and turns back, presenting the *Singapore Song* with a crisp salute. Then he turns and dives into the water, surfacing twenty feet closer to shore.

When he reaches the ramp he walks up it toward us, his soaked clothes clinging to his angular frame. Somehow he even still has his hat. His face is slack, his eyes seemingly unseeing, and I suddenly think of a neighbor of ours whose house caught fire and burned in the middle of a torpid Sunday afternoon. My father's numb expression is the same one I saw on that man's face as the fire trucks arrived—too late, as it turned out—all those years ago.

"Are you hurt?" my mom asks him.

"I lost it," he says. "It's gone. All of it."

"Oh honey," she says. She puts her arms around his midsection and pulls him in close.

"I'm soaked," he says.

"Yes," she says. "I know."

"I lost it all," he says again. "What am I gonna do now?"

"Build another. Build it again. Even better this time."

My father seems to consider it seriously for a moment or two. Then he shakes his head, firmly and forcefully. "I could," he says, "but I can't."

I look away and pretend he's not crying.

●

The boat cannot be moved, not yet. The tide is too high to get a trailer to it.

"I can't just wait around here for eight hours," my father tells the bystanders. He jerks a thumb at us. "These kids will go nuts." He'll drop us off at home and return around six p.m., he says. The tide should be low enough then, but not so low as to make it impossible to re-trailer the boat. Several of the beachgoers offer to help when he comes back.

"If you're still here, yes, that would be great," he says. His voice is muted and flat, and I wonder where that tent-preacher's energy, that three-ring showmanship he had on display an hour ago, has gone. "Don't hang around on my account though." But I know my father. I know he'll never come back for that boat, that he'll probably just call in an anonymous report to the Coast Guard or the Harbor Patrol or whoever would handle this sort of thing. Or maybe he'll just let it rot where it lies.

Either way, I know we will never speak of the *Singapore Song* again. The test was a failure, the day was a failure, the project a failure. All we know is that it was a leak that brought down the *Singapore Song*, that it opened quickly, and that now he has nothing at all to show for the last five months of his life. We do not know if it was because of the dump truck that almost ran us off the road this morning, or because the materials weren't up to the job, or because my father's boatbuilding ambitions and requirements outpaced his skills. Maybe if he'd started smaller, he could have built something seaworthy. But he needed something big enough for all four of us, something that could carry us all far from his disappointment and frustration, even though we are at least partly the cause of it.

"Hey," my mom says to my father once we've been on the road for ten minutes or so. "Do you want to talk about . . . well, anything?"

"No," he says curtly. "But thanks for asking."

"I know you probably don't want to hear this right now," she says, "but this was a good experience for you."

"Uh huh," he says, and I can hear his eyes rolling just in his tone. "Gimme a break, willya?"

"I know money's tight. But this was *good* for you, and I—"

"It was a fucking failure and so am I," he says.

In the rearview mirror, I see him wrench up his face into a sour grimace, like he just tasted raw sewage, and then without warning he swerves out of the lane and up onto the shoulder.

Traffic rumbles past. We are silent; my father just sits there, staring straight ahead. And then he is up and out, slamming the door behind him. "Grady, what—" my mom calls after him, but he is already on the other side of traffic, standing in the median and watching the oncoming cars.

"Mom, what is he doing?" I ask.

"I'm watching the same thing you are," she says.

Then my father rips the captain's hat from his head, spins around like an Olympic hammer-thrower, and heaves the cap into traffic. An oncoming semi-truck immediately chews it up in its massive tires and spits it out the back end.

"Everyone get this through your heads, because I don't want to hear about it again," he says when he's back in the Volaré. "My captaining days are over." Something in his voice tells me that this is not his low point yet, that things will still have to get worse for him before they can get better. But how can it get worse? He has lost so much of himself already. He is a different man than he was in those early days of unemployment, when he'd beat everyone to the breakfast table, fully dressed and already blitzing his way through the day's want ads with his red felt-tip; he's emptier now, more desperate. I realize I do not know this person in the driver's seat of our family car; his presence there unnerves me.

We ride the rest of the way home in silence. Jack leans his head against the window and naps. I watch from the back seat as my mom moves to gently rest her hand on her husband's forearm, to offer him what little she can while he drives. But it's too late. She can't reach him; the current is just too strong.

When the Drought Finally Ends

"Let's pretend we have a million dollars," she whispers in your ear as you climb the stairs that lead to yet another seven-figure-pricetag Mission District down-to-the-studs, bleach-white-modern renovation job. You nod because, for reasons you don't quite understand, you are only too willing to pretend this really is your life, to pretend there is already a *we* after spending just a couple of hours together, to pretend anything she wants.

"Okay," you whisper back. "We'll say I'm an astronaut, and you invented the hashtag."

The condo is steeped in the soft natural light coming in from the big front windows that look out onto an open dumpster, and beyond that, to Zeitgeist, where until ten minutes ago the two of you downed lazy first-date beers in the sun while everything around you—the bikers, the tourists, the anarchic punk rock on the jukebox—seemed to fall away somehow, leaving just you and her in your own impenetrable pocket of reality. The view out the back is directly into another condo. The listing agent doesn't seem to know what to make of you, can't quite figure out if he should treat you like serious prospects or just another pair of tourists from Walnut Creek. So he probes.

"So what do you do for work? You guys in tech?"

"We step in front of cars and sue the drivers," she says. "It's pretty lucrative, but it gets kind of physically demanding after a while, so we have to work as a team."

"Uh huh, I see. So. Um. Do you have kids?"

"Well . . . not anymore," she says, and she shoots you a conspiratorial glance. The listing agent retreats into his brochures. There are no more questions.

"This could be your room, honey," you hear her call to you from the second bedroom. "Look." She slides open a closet door. "Plenty of room to lean at night."

"Maybe I could get a hammock," you say.

"No hammocks," she says. "I'm not having you drill holes in my million-dollar walls."

On the bus ride to her apartment, there are no seats. You both stand in the aisle of the number 14, pressed against each other, making out the entire length of Mission Street in the middle of the day. People push past you, all elbows and backpacks and judgment, but they cannot dislodge your mouth from hers.

On the street, the high winds whip her hair up and around. It floats and jabs and reaches out to caress you. It stings like nettles when it pricks you in the eyes. "I'm a hot mess," she says, and she holds onto you like she worries the wind might scoop her up and carry her off at any moment.

"Don't you ever leave me," she says.

"I won't if you don't," you say back.

It is your best day yet.

It's the day that changes everything.

●

This is your fifth month in San Francisco. This is the city you've chosen. It's streaked in filth and graffiti and shit, awash in pretense and possibility, sticky with money. It's sparkling identical steel-and-glass towers bursting out of the ground and blotting out the past with their long shadows, sprouting so quickly that the pavement has no time to heal before the next one germinates. It's tucked-away staircases and secret garden spaces high atop the hills. It's jackets in the middle of July. It's the raw sewage stench of mid-Market. It's authenticity and artifice, energy and inertia, searing passion and stark indifference all at once.

And you want so badly to love it, to love the living *shit* out of it, to love it so much you become part of it yourself.

This all sounded like a great idea back when you first had it, driving three thousand miles to live out a half-considered dream a full continent away from where you'd spent the vast majority of your previous days. Picking up and moving to San Francisco on little more than a whim is the kind of thing that almost sounds like an actual accomplishment if you don't think about it too hard. Like winning a hot dog eating contest, or shooting your mouth off at someone famous and getting away with it, or finishing grad school.

But the city turned out to be cold, and not just in the summer. It snubbed every effort you made to get close to it. For the longest time, your very first thought after waking up in the morning was of leaving. Every day. Buy a plane ticket for that afternoon and just go, get the hell out. No gear, no baggage, no nothing. Just whatever you were wearing at that exact moment. Write the rest of it off as the cost of living your own decisions.

But that wouldn't work, because there was nowhere to go, no place to hide where you could convincingly reinvent yourself as someone who hadn't failed at everything he ever tried to do, someone who could decide what he wanted and go get it, someone who could formulate a plan and work it through to the end.

Hell, you wouldn't even know how to *pretend* to be that. Let alone actually *be* it.

Then it was suddenly all moot, because that was when you swiped right on her profile in that stupid shallow app you hated but used anyway because, hey, you never know, right? It totally could happen this time.

Then you promptly forgot all about it.

When—much to your surprise—she reciprocated three days later, it was with the tersest of paragraphs: *Beers @ Zeitgeist, one hour from right now. Deleting this profile in 59 min. This is your only chance.*

And that's all it took: you were hooked, reeled in and halfway in the boat before you even left your apartment.

Dead man walking.

●

Sex and breakfast. That's what you smell like when you walk her back to her place in the mornings. That smell, coating the palm of your hand, lodged deep in the ridges and whorls of your fingerprints, under your nails.

Every time you kiss her at her door, it's like you still hunger, like breakfast was nothing but air and sunlight, like the sweaty sleepless night you just had actually happened months ago, or maybe to someone else. Then it's back through the Mission and down to the BART station, and when you pass by, Cesar Chavez complains about the drought. Every fucking time.

This drought, baby, he says to you. *I'm losing my mind. The sidewalks stink like bum piss. It's too much. Can't you get someone to, you know, do something about it? For me? You* must *know someone with a hose.*

The snowman around the corner, he's more direct. *This city's a goddamn toilet,* he always says. *Always has been. It smells like the polar bear exhibit at the zoo.*

Somehow, it doesn't seem strange to you that the murals talk. Maybe they talk to everyone. That's probably it.

You think about how she likes to burrow herself into that space under your arm in the middle of the night. How she drapes a lithe arm across your chest and calls you *smush.* Softly, like she's singing it, right into your ear. And you. Just. *Soar.* None of the various substances you've dumped into your bloodstream over the course of your entire life have ever made you feel like *that.*

The days are different now. The city is no longer quite so impenetrable and unknowable. It no longer looms over you, intimidating you, no longer thwarts you at every turn. Its mysteries reveal themselves, almost in a flood, because she knows them all, knows what's behind every door, knows all the secrets that live in plain sight on every next block.

You take the steps down into the station two at a time and bounce right past the busker with the cracked violin, rasping and creaking away at the fog-eyed morning commuters. Sex and breakfast. It follows you all day. You savor it, lifting your shirt collar to your nose and breathing it deep, not caring how people on the train look at you, all of them probably haters anyway, probably not getting any themselves. Oh man, that *scent*. Why would you ever want to shake it?

●

Something you've noticed: Everything in this city is uphill. Downhill is just a cruel illusion. There is no down. Not after scaling those hills, climbing those endless steps, riding those boundless highs. And even if you could go back down, why would you? You've seen that already. Lived it. Felt it—or rather, *not* felt it, because there is no rush down there, no burn, no cascade of endorphins exploding through you, nothing to feel.

And you swear to yourself that you're never going back, not ever, because higher is better.

Except sometimes, higher is impossible. Sometimes you're already as high as you can go. And you might not even know it.

●

Sometimes you skip work to see her in the middle of the day. She never closes her bedroom windows, never draws the curtains. Anyone could just see in. You wonder how far her noises carry down the alley behind her building. You wonder how many of her neighbors already know your name.

But sometimes you come by and she's not home. Even if she knew you were coming. You stand there and press the buzzer, press it again, press it again. This time you hold it. This time you lean into it and try to push it straight through the panel and into the wall. You text. *I'm here. Where r u?*

No answer.

Maybe she's in the shower.

She's not in the shower. You know this. But you let yourself pretend to believe it anyway.

Expectations are landmines, the black-and-white paisley tiger tells you as you pass by on your way back to the BART station.

I don't have any expectations, you tell it.

Then what are you even doing here? it asks, and you have no answer for that.

●

Something you've noticed: She only tells you the truth when you're inside her.

"I don't remember your name."

"I can't care about you."

"I am trying to drive you away."

"I will destroy you if you let me."

It's all the other times when you can't tell, when truth is just a coin flip. "You keep me sane," she says, and you love hearing that so you believe it, because if you believe it maybe she'll say it again. "Don't make out with any other girls," she says as you try to pull yourself away one morning, and she bites your lower lip hard enough to make it bleed. "I can get pretty jealous."

You taste copper for the rest of the day. You work that sore spot on your lip between your front teeth, just hard enough to remind you of that morning's buffet, and of what's waiting for you after work. The dull pain of it sets your heart racing.

But when you come by that afternoon, she doesn't answer her buzzer.

Everything is uphill here.

Mark my words, the snowman says as you pass by. *One day, the chickens will come home to roost.*

And when they do, you say, I will kill them and eat them. Think about *that*, chickens, before you come back here.

The snowman laughs at your bravado. You wonder if he can tell how full of shit you are.

Boy, that woman of yours, Cesar says to you later. *I see her walking around here sometimes. You know she plays at proletariat, but she's bourgeoisie down to her core.*

Come on, Cesar. We've talked about respecting boundaries before, remember? Besides, what does that even mean?

I don't know, man. I just thought it sounded good.

Dude, you don't even know her.

Maybe not, he says, *but neither do you.*

●

You start this morning by looking in the mirror and saying "I don't love you anymore." Over and over. You did this yesterday too. And the day before.

Who are you talking to? Her? The *last* her? Here?

Yourself?

Maybe.

That night you lay on the living room floor, both of you naked and spent. She pulls your hand up to her chest and rests it flat across her sternum. "This is for you," she says. "It's yours, to use however you see fit."

You say nothing, press your hand down a little more firmly.

"I'm putting my heart in your hands," she says. "Don't you want it?"

"Of course I do," you say. "More than anything. I just . . . can't seem to find it. Hang on."

But before you can, she pushes your hand away, quickly sliding it down the length of her body. "Then I guess you'll just have to keep looking," she says.

You watch her as she gets up and moves to open the window, and for a moment she is a silhouette, flawless in line and form, backlit by the placid nighttime lights high above in Dolores Heights. She holds herself there for a moment, between you and the city beyond, and you can't tell whether she is observing or displaying. You reach for her, wanting to pull her back down on top of you, but your depth perception is faulty in the dark. Everything is farther away than it looks, much farther.

"I think you're destroying me," you tell her. "I think I'm letting you do it."

She gets down on all fours and crawls over to you, climbs up onto your chest. "And I bet it feels incredible."

●

Maybe it's the wrong apartment, you think. Maybe I pressed the wrong button. You try three more times, because you never know, maybe the panel's wiring is crossed, or maybe you're reading the numbers on the buttons wrong—hers *is* 227, right?—or maybe she has guests or something.

Suddenly the front door swings open—it's an old lady heading out to walk her overly primped little dog. Not who you were hoping for, but she'll do, because the instant she turns the corner, you grab the door just before it locks itself shut again and slip inside the building.

Up two flights, down the hall to the left. Her door is standing wide open.

"*Estas jodidamente loco,*" a man's voice says from inside the apartment as you're walking up. You square yourself with the doorframe and peer inside the place, now both empty of all traces of her and completely trashed: deep gouges in the floor. Holes in the wall where chunks of drywall have been yanked out. A black, tar-like substance smeared over the walls. Dirt from smashed flowerpots all over the floor. Windows broken. Toilet tank lid cracked in two porcelain halves, resting on the kitchen linoleum.

It's a complete shitshow.

"The fuck you want?" one of the men says to you. There are three of them, two of whom smoke cigarettes and all of whom are Latino, wearing overalls and work gloves. A giant trash can sits in the middle of the living room.

"Hey," another one says. "You know the bitch who lives here?"

"She gotta pay for all this," the first one says. "Look what she did."

"You know where she went? Come on, man."

"Someone's gotta pay for what she did."

It's not the wrong apartment. You are just in the wrong place now. She is gone.

Just like that.

"You're not supposed to smoke in here," is all you can think of to say to them before leaving.

Numb, you wander through the Mission for hours, past all the sticky dive bars and grimy taquerias and the towering heaps of garbage and detritus. Fragments of thoughts stream into your head, winking into and out of existence far too quickly for your mind to pluck out any one of them and examine it. All you can do is walk. One foot forward. Then the other. It's the most complex process you can manage.

Haven't seen her, the snowman says. *Sorry.*

I don't care, you say. I don't care if I never see her again.

She's gotta be around here somewhere, Cesar says. *Don't worry, you'll find her.*

But I'm not looking for her, you protest. I'm just . . . walking.

Okay, Cesar says. *Sure, man. Whatever you say.*

You mind? You're standing on my face, Lou Reed complains.

You step to an adjoining section of sidewalk. Sorry, Lou.

You ache. Your lungs won't fill all the way. Your stomach is full of hummingbirds. You want to scream, *need* to scream. Why can't you scream?

Listen, Super Mario says as you pass, and of course you *do* listen, you stop everything and listen because you've known Super Mario since you were seven and he has never steered you wrong. *Stop feeling so sorry for yourself. This city, it does not care about you. It's just a collection of buildings and streets and strangers. It's entirely indifferent to whether you exist or not. It doesn't even know you're here. It won't notice when you leave.*

Maybe for most people, sure, you say. But I belong here. It's different.

No, man, Mario says. *That's a front.*

This place, Luigi chimes in. *Man, it will change your life. It'll change you. But it won't fix a damn thing for you, not even the things you didn't know you brought. Maybe even especially those. You dig?*

She didn't even exist for you two months ago, Mario adds. *So what have you lost?*

I don't know, you say. But something.

●

The buses are all wrong somehow, making turns they shouldn't, leaving you adrift in uncharted distant neighborhoods. Everything is without texture. There is no reason to do anything. You are in the wrong place.

You have been scrubbed from her digital life. Dropped from Facebook. Unfollowed on Instagram. Blocked on Twitter. The 21st century equivalent of doctoring newspaper photos to remove out-of-favor party apparatchiks.

You've been un-personed.

Fine then, you think. All you can do is delete her from your phone. Which you do, but the act feels hollow. It has no emancipating power. Besides, you still remember her phone number. It's the only one you've memorized in the last fifteen years.

Eventually, you text her. Even though you promised yourself you wouldn't, that you'd leave her alone until she came back to you, no matter how long that took. That promise was immediately followed by another, that you wouldn't be too hard on yourself when you inevitably failed to keep the first promise. At least you know you'll keep the second.

Where did u go?

What happened?

I'm worried

I miss u. Plz come back. Wherever u r

But no replies come. Until one finally does, weeks later, at 10:37 on a Wednesday morning.

It reads: *Who is this?*

●

The day you leave is the day the drought ends. The smudged ash sky over San Francisco rips open, as if the point of the Transamerica Pyramid has torn a great gash along its underbelly, and the rain is suddenly there again, like a long-lost deadbeat brother. Afternoon traffic slips and snarls and throbs on the 101 as months of caked-on oils and lubricants are suddenly stirred from their bone-dry beds, soaked loose and free and now streaking their way along the pavement, twisting beneath the cars in shimmering ribbons of delicate toxins. The jabbering voices on the radio are giddy with disbelief. Rain. Rain. *Rain!*

This is the last time you will ever hear my voice, she never said to you. *I thought it was only fair to tell you that.* You can almost, *almost* hear her say the words in your mind. She is starting to dissolve. You're already forgetting what she looks like.

There's always Austin, you think. But you've tried that already. Austin was the sweet girl from down the street who you flirted with for a couple years but never did quite fall in love with, no matter how hard you tried.

Still. It's not a bad second choice. It could work this time.

Or maybe not, because you have to actually get there first. A sea of cars hems you in, all of them immobilized by the unexpected rain and the chaos it has brought. This, you realize, was to be expected. After all, nothing is actually *easy* about this place. Everything takes more money, more time, more planning, more shoving, just *more*—until one day, there *is* no more, you have nothing left to give and so you leave your thirty-six-hundred-a-month studio apartment for the next sucker standing in line, freshly scrubbed and just in from Tempe, already drowning before he even knows it's happening.

It takes more than just a single deluge to end a drought. There is no reason to think the next day will bring more rain, or the next, or that this is anything more than just a momentary disruption of the dry spell.

That stupid paisley tiger was right, you think.

But for now you sit and wait, for nature and the people in front of you to get their collective shit together, because you couldn't turn around now even if you wanted to. There are too many landmines back there.

Let someone else trip them now.

Hugo

At nine years old, I have heard the story of how Daniel Foley lost his eye at least a hundred times but I have still never seen Hugo. He's there, though. He lives in his cave dug out of the backside of the biggest hill on the grounds at day camp. He is probably a troll. He has definitely eaten unwary campers before. But that hasn't happened for a while, not since I started coming here. This does not make me feel safer. Instead it makes me think how hungry he must be.

Jenny is tall, like a grownup almost. She has wild blonde hair and can do anything. She has read all the Choose Your Own Adventure books. Everyone is in love with her. Especially me. Jenny does not believe in Hugo. She tucks the corner of her mouth up into her cheek at the mention of his name. I pretend to disbelieve too, when I'm around her. I would probably die if she ever rolled her eyes at me.

"You kids stay out of there," Ellen says whenever we talk about the cave, which is pretty much all the time. She sounds distracted whenever she talks to us, like she is re-ordering a mental list of all the places she'd rather be than here.

We can't *not* talk about the cave. But talk is as far as it goes. Nobody I know of has ever been inside it. Except, of course, for Daniel Foley, who went in there once and came out with a stick jammed deep into his eyeball. You could hear his howling through the solid oak doors of the infirmary and halfway down the big hill.

That was years ago. I wasn't a camper here then and I have never met Daniel, if he is even real. But Shannon swears he is, she's friends with Daniel's cousin and he still wears an eyepatch, a constant reminder of his arrogance in seeking out what should never be seen, and of Hugo's terrible mercy.

Tonight is sleepover night for my group. We have one every couple of weeks. There's always a campfire big enough to be a Viking funeral pyre, s'mores, night swimming, all the usual things. Simone will probably sing "Tainted Love" and pound away at her acoustic guitar again. Counselors are always doing things like that, trying to prove to themselves they aren't old yet.

Of course, on these nights the now-empty camp is suddenly full of possibility and dread, a wide-open expanse full of hills and forest and trails and dark corners. It's far too much territory for just the twenty of us to control: during the day, our sheer numbers keep Hugo contained. But at night the camp is his. At night it would be a trivial thing to disappear into the woods of birch and red oak, to take a wrong turn down a quiet path that leads only to a grisly end. We must stick together, or be lost.

After dinner Jenny and I play box hockey until after sunset. My rules are onesies, because my game is defense.

Whenever Jenny wins she calls a scramble, which really means no rules, just hacking away at the plywood puck. Thwack-thwack-thwack. She is athletic, as strong as any of the boys in our group, and often overpowers me in scrambles. We drop the puck over and over. I wish time would stop.

But she looks up and around. "Where is everyone?"

She's right. We're alone in the suddenly ominous dusk, just her and me. And Hugo. We do not see him but he is there, watching, waiting, hungry.

"Now's our chance," she says. "Let's go see Hugo."

"I thought you didn't believe in Hugo," I say.

"I don't. I want to find out what everyone's so scared of."

We bring our box hockey sticks with us. The path to Hugo's cave takes us around the big hill and along the edge of the woods, where there are no lights. Like everyone else, I know the way. The cave is a magnet for us; we've all been right up to it, daring each other to get closer, get *closer*, one step further I dare you. How close can you get before you lose your nerve? We treat it like a game, but we only play it when the sun is shining.

I steal a quick glance at Jenny; the light is fading now but I can still see her face, and as I am staring she turns to look at me, and she smiles. I weigh the relative pros and cons of losing my nerve in front of Jenny on the one hand, and being eaten by Hugo on the other. It is not an obvious choice.

Her expression changes as the cave comes into view. I can sense her natural confidence dissipate like bubbles from ginger ale. I grip my box hockey stick like a club. It's heavy and comforting. She digs her fingers into my arm. Jenny will never admit her fear. She will never admit that Hugo is real, even as he devours us whole, his breath tangy and rotten, his fangs sharp and inevitable. For the first time, I feel like a man, even though I'm terrified.

We are standing outside the mouth of the cave now. I listen for the sound of Hugo breathing, the deep rumbling of his stomach. But I hear only the crickets and the beating of my own heart. I fish my tiny squeezable flashlight out of my pocket—it's the kind that's supposed to go on a keyring, but I don't have any keys—point it into the cave and squeeze. But we're still too far away, and the light dies before it reaches the cave.

"It's pretty dark in there," she says. I can't tell if she is sounding me out for a joint retreat or testing my resolve: will I yield or will I persevere?

"Let's go in together," I say.

"You first," she says. "I'll be right behind you."

"This was your idea."

"You're the one with the flashlight."

Of course it was always going to come to this. "Fine," I say, and I step toward the cave, my stick pointed straight out in front of me, the muscles in my arm quivering. I take another step, and another, and another. I am closer to the cave than I have ever been. I close my eyes and take another step. I do not allow myself to think about what I am doing or why I am doing it because I don't understand either the *what* or the *why* and I still don't hear anything from inside the cave. I hold my breath and I take another step and then another and I open my eyes and I'm surrounded by darkness, a dank and hideous darkness.

"Your flashlight!" Jenny calls from outside the cave. She stands exactly where I left her.

I dig the flashlight out again and squeeze. This time it's dark enough. But there are no bones strewn about, no bloodied sneakers to warn off hapless intruders. Just a dozen or so rusted-out classroom desks tipped onto their sides. An old coffee maker in the back. Hockey sticks, cracked and splintered and unusable. Moldy cardboard boxes filled to overflowing with glass bottles. A rolled-up carpet with stains around the edge. A ten-speed bicycle missing its front wheel.

Junk storage. That's all this is. That's what we've been so afraid of all this time.

"Just a bunch of shitty desks in here," I yell to Jenny. "Some other junk too. You can come in. You were right. Hugo's not real."

I turn around to call to her again, in case she didn't hear me. But Jenny is not there.

I am alone, in Hugo's cave, at night, and I am not afraid.

I find her with everyone else about twenty minutes later, in the cluster of pastel domes where the little kids do gymnastics. Simone is threading the projector when I walk in—*ohhhhhh right*, the movie. I'd forgotten.

"Those aren't allowed in here," Simone says. I look down. I still have the stick. Everyone is looking at me except for Jenny, who is sitting with the girls on the far side of the dome, where boys are not welcome. I sit with my own kind instead.

Nobody asks where I've been. They wouldn't believe me anyway.

FANTASTIC ATLAS

I don't believe in carry-on luggage. I used to carry everything on with me when I flew anywhere, but all the traveling I've done over the last twelve years has altered my way of seeing things. My new philosophy is, when you travel, you should take advantage of every convenience they offer you. The entire process of flying— busy airports and crowded planes and endless lines at customs—is trying enough in the best of circumstances. Why would you want to endure any more exasperation than necessary by toting your luggage with you the whole way?

The only exception is the atlas. That always comes with me on the plane. I never check it, never even pack it. Atlas under the seat in front of me, purse in my lap. I don't like to let it out of my sight. But it sometimes doesn't fit under the seat, and when I have to put it in the overhead compartment I always end up fretting about it for the entire flight. I rarely get much sleep on those flights.

Today, however, it does fit.

At least, it fits for this leg of the trip. I'll have to change planes twice. First in Seattle, then again in Frankfurt. I usually don't like to do that but it was the best I could do this time. It's been a tight year.

I've never been to Italy before. My mother was happy to hear that I was finally going to see our ancestral homeland with my own eyes, even though she doesn't generally approve of my reasons for doing all this traveling. A waste of time, she thinks. She'd be disappointed if she knew I wasn't planning to get up to Brescia at all. That's where our people are. But you never know. Lucca isn't all that far.

●

By the time Zachary made his first map, he hadn't said a word to anyone in well over a year. Actually, it was closer to one year, seven months and thirteen days, give or take an hour or two. Which was long after Warren had left, an important detail that never seemed to register with Doctor Behrendt. I had to tell him at least four times before it sunk in.

He'd barely even had time to learn to talk before he gave it up. I wanted to know why, wanted that more than anything. How had I failed him? Maybe if I knew, I could do something about it.

That map, though. You should have seen it—or, rather, you should have seen him draw it, since the map itself was essentially just a line. He did it in a single sitting and completely from memory, with the free-flowing confidence of a master cartographer. I will never forget him in that moment, sitting at the kitchen table, his little legs kicking back and forth as he worked, his mouth set tight in concentration.

What is *this?* I remember thinking when he handed it to me, but of course I knew what it was right away: It was a map of the bus route we used to take to get from our flat in Potrero Hill to my mother's apartment up in Presidio Heights, the 33. He had precisely scaled and plotted each turn and run of roadway. He didn't label any of the streets, but he didn't have to; that route was as familiar to me as the sound of my own breathing.

"Did you draw this?" I asked him, even though I had literally just watched him do exactly that. He just looked back at me, silent, a vaguely insulted expression on his face.

It was a dumb question. But he was only six years old. Something like this should have been well beyond his reach. I gave the entire kitchen a once-over to see if there might be an old Muni map lying around, anything for him to copy from. There wasn't.

"How did you do that?" But of course he wasn't going to tell me. He just smiled, and I knew I would have to be satisfied with that, because it was all I was going to get.

●

I showed the map to Doctor Behrendt at our next session. I didn't have much else to talk about, really; everything was pretty much the same as it had ever been. He held up the map so that the afternoon sunlight from the office's only window was directly behind it, as if he was looking for a watermark. Then he took off his glasses and absently polished a lens with the hem of his sweater.

"This is a good sign," he announced.

"Is it?"

"Oh yes," he said. "Very promising. Don't you think so?"

I shrugged. "Honestly, I don't know anymore. At this point, I don't trust my own judgment."

"I think we are getting close. Give him some encouragement. Maybe he will start talking soon."

Oh. *Encouragement.* Is *that* the answer, then. Why on earth didn't you say so before, doctor?

I had been offering nothing but encouragement for one year, seven months, and eighteen days. I didn't want to offer any more encouragement. I was tired of encouraging. I was tired of a lot of things.

And I was *definitely* too tired to stop at a CVS on the way home to pick up a ruler, a box of colored pencils, and a thick tablet of cheap drawing paper. But I did it anyway. Not because I was optimistic; I hadn't been optimistic in months. I did it because—even though it probably wouldn't be, even though I *knew* it wouldn't be—what if this was finally the thing that worked, that just clicked everything right back into place?

What if I gave up and turned out to be wrong?

But you know, the truth is that I'd probably never have known the difference. Everything would have just gone on exactly as it was. I'd still have Zachary. He'd still have me. And that could have been enough for me, even if he never spoke so much as a single word for the rest of his life.

I could have just stopped. I could have rested. I *could* have.

Maybe I should have.

Maybe I was stupid for persisting.
Maybe I still am.

●

The elderly man in the seat next to me is lonely. It's easy to tell; he has that look of someone who is desperate for conversation. He takes advantage of the moment when my earbuds are out, just after I take them out to order a glass of wine from the flight attendant. He tells me he is going to Copenhagen, retracing the steps of a trip he took decades ago with his late wife. I tell him I am going to Italy for the first time.

"Oh, how ex*cit*ing," he says. "Are you traveling alone?"

"I'm visiting my son," I tell him.

"That's wonderful. Is he a student?"

I smile and give a half-nod. Neither a yes nor a no.

"I do love Italy. One of my favorite destinations. Will you be getting up to Lake Como at all?"

"Oh, I doubt we'll have time," I say, and I look back toward the rear of the plane. "I'm sorry, can you excuse me for a moment?" I ask, and I stand, as if I've been waiting for the all-clear light on one of the restrooms the entire time.

"Of course," he says. I pick up the atlas and head back. I don't usually like talking to people about my travels. I definitely don't like talking to strangers about Zachary.

I wait in the restroom for five minutes or so. While I'm in there, I take the atlas from its bag and leaf through it, occasionally stopping to trace a finger along a jagged zigzag of scotch tape down the center. Not all the maps have one of these. But more of them do than don't.

I still don't know where all these places are supposed to be. I have a theory that I can't prove, which is that some of them don't exist anymore. And that others don't exist *yet*.

When I return to my seat, the elderly man is asleep. I put my earbuds back in, take a sip of wine, and close my eyes, clutching the atlas tight in my arms.

●

At the time, I just thought of it as Zachary's maps phase. Like other kids go through a dinosaur phase or a princess phase. It was all he seemed to want to do, from the moment he'd get up in the morning. I used to have to put his colored pencils on top of the fridge to get him to stop long enough to eat his dinner, which he would always just wolf down in a few fierce bites, one eye on the pencil box the entire time.

They were simple at first. He mapped out our usual Sunday afternoon walking route through Golden Gate Park. There was one that turned out to be a map of his school. It included rooms he shouldn't have known about, janitorial storage rooms and admin offices tucked away well behind the reception desk. I made a mental note to ask someone at the school about that.

It wasn't long before he started mapping entire cities. The San Francisco peninsula was first. It took him an entire Sunday to do that one. Then he did the island of Manhattan after school the next day.

But there were others too, maps of places I didn't know, these strange spiderwebs of streets, sometimes bisected by an oxbow of some rambling waterway. I took one of those with me to work and James, our map librarian, told me he was pretty sure it was Cincinnati.

"Maybe he copied it from an atlas at school," Doctor Behrendt suggested at our next session.

"That doesn't make any sense," I said. "Copying isn't his style. And even if it was, why would he pick Cincinnati? He's never been there."

He shrugged. "With any luck, you can ask him that yourself soon."

On my way home, it occurred to me just how much therapy relies on well-placed platitudes. *It's a good sign. Give it some time. It's about the journey, not the destination. He'll talk when he's ready.*

What a load of horseshit it all is. How's *that* for a platitude?

Maybe it was time to drop therapy for good. The only person who seemed to get anything out of it was Doctor Behrendt. It felt like it had stopped working for me a while ago, and I was pretty sure it hadn't helped Zachary at all.

But he *was* communicating, in his way. I couldn't deny that. Understanding would come. Words would follow, maybe, but for the moment, I had to make do with maps: dozens of them, all rendered with a level of detail that should have been impossible for a kid his age.

We taped them all up on his bedroom wall, starting with the map of San Francisco. He hung that next to his blue dresser and directly above his Adventure Time nightlight. For some reason, it comforted me that he'd chosen that particular map to honor with pride of place. Maybe it was a sign that Zachary understood where he was from, where his people had made their lives for four generations. But we quickly surrounded it with other maps, mostly of places I didn't know. They eventually sprawled across the entire wall. With each new map he added, the display's center of gravity shifted, gradually creeping toward the doorway, and soon home wasn't at the center of anything anymore.

●

When Zachary was two, maybe three, I used to spend long nights watching the fog ruffle and shimmer under the streetlights outside his bedroom window, listening to him toss and turn in his bed for an hour or so until he would finally sink into sleep.

I always blamed myself for his restlessness. I still don't know why, but I did. That's why I would sit with him for so long. I was doing penance.

Back then I was still getting used to it being just Zachary and me. After sitting with him for a while, my thoughts would usually turn to the one subject I couldn't seem to just let alone, which was How Things Used To Be. Nothing good ever came of these ruminations. But I kept going back to them, working them like a garden that would never give back anything but dandelion greens and kudzu.

Warren had never talked much either. Just enough to let me know I'd failed.

I used to wonder if Zachary would get the chance to know his father after all. Eventually that shifted, and I would wonder instead if Zachary would *remember* him. But mostly I just hoped he wouldn't think to ask about the man.

●

When I thought Zachary had started stealing, the only thing I did about it was mention it to Doctor Behrendt. That doesn't really count as doing something, though. Maybe I should have confronted Zachary about it directly.

The first thing I found was the egg. It was in Zachary's dresser drawer, protected by a soft blockade of sock rolls, and it looked ceramic but wasn't. It was a real egg that had been emptied, hollowed out through a tiny hole in the bottom and then painted with a fine-tipped brush in intricate interlocking patterns of crimson, gold and black enamel. I almost broke it when I picked it up because I was expecting it to have some heft.

He obviously didn't make it himself; he certainly couldn't afford to buy something like that. Maybe it came from one of his teachers.

Oh, and about a week before that, I found what appeared to be a bus transfer from Buenos Aires in the pockets of one of his pairs of jeans. The transfer was three days old; I assumed he just picked it up off the street somewhere. I remember lecturing him about it. *Do you have any idea how filthy this city is? I don't care if it's a twenty-dollar bill. If you find it on the ground, leave it there. How many times do I have to tell you that?* The whole time Zachary's eyes did not leave the thin paper strip. He homed in on it like a mongoose tracking a bird, until it was close enough for him to snatch right out of my hand. He darted into his room and slammed the door before I could even react.

I put the egg back in its hiding place and closed the drawer. I should call the school, I thought, but I decided to wait until I figured out a tactful way to approach it. Then, about a month later and after I'd forgotten all about it, I found seven small coins in Zachary's room. They were stamped in a language I could not read and bore the faces of statesmen I did not recognize. Zachary had lined them up neatly on his windowsill, right next to the headboard of his bed. They were obviously old; the edges were nicked and unevenly worn, and the almost imperious dignity of the buffed metal was undone here and there with tiny pinpoints of oxidation.

I checked his dresser again for the egg but it was gone. I might have managed to convince myself that I'd imagined it if not for the coins.

"That is not unusual for children his age," Doctor Behrendt said when I told him about it. He wrote something down in his notebook. I was suddenly certain that he'd been doodling all these months instead of taking notes. "What makes you think that is what he has been up to?"

"I found some things in his room. Things that I don't know where they came from." And I told him about the egg and the coins and the bus transfer.

"I expect he will grow out of this," he said when I was finished.

I gave him a hard stare. Should I tell him about how I found Zachary in bed the other morning with mud caked in his hair and gravel in his pajama pockets? About the dirt that was streaked and ground into his sheets, but somehow absent from the cream-colored rug in the middle of the room? About how *different* Zachary had seemed in that moment, and the certainty I'd been having that he was looking at *me* differently now too?

No. I'd keep that to myself. Instead I just rolled my eyes. "That seems to be your answer for everything lately."

"Nevertheless." He wrote something else, just three or four strokes of his pen. I imagined him sketching a simple line drawing: maybe a dog, or a sailboat, or a penis. "I still would not worry too much. He is definitely trying to say something. See if he's ready to draw something else."

"Drawing isn't talking," I shot back. "Neither is stealing."

"They are both means of communication, in their own ways. One step at a time."

"More platitudes. How very zen of you." I got up to leave.

"Our session is not over yet."

"I don't think this is helping anymore. And to be blunt, I don't know if it ever helped."

"Of course it is. You may not see it, but I do."

I sighed. "When will I be able to stop taking your word for it?"

●

In the Frankfurt airport I stop at a kiosk for a beer and a sandwich. The sign is mostly in German, which I don't speak, but towards the bottom there is a phrase in English: *Eat the right feeling*.

Now *there's* a platitude for you.

Maybe that's why therapy hasn't helped. Maybe I've just been eating the wrong feelings this whole time.

The terminal is busy but not especially crowded. I find myself idly scoping out the other travelers as they pass by. Force of habit, mostly. I don't actually expect to see him here. As far as I've been able to tell, he never drew a map of Frankfurt.

I arrive at my gate early, nearly an hour before boarding is scheduled to begin. Bright sunshine flows in through the windows overlooking the runway. It looks like early afternoon outside; my body has not adjusted to the new time zone, and so my internal clock is completely useless. I don't have anything to read to kill the time, so I haul out the stack of Zachary's maps and start leafing through them.

There are so many.

Sometimes he did three or four in a single day. After a while they all began to blur together. By then I had long since stopped thinking of them as some kind of hopeful development, or as an intermediate stage he was passing through on his way to talking again. They started to feel more like mockery, an act of withholding from me the very thing he knew I needed most. Like he was just shoving that fact in my face.

I tried to steer him to other things instead. Like the neighbor's house, the fuchsia-lavender-and-mustard

Victorian directly across the street. "Why not draw that?" I asked him. "Look at those colors. Wouldn't that be a beautiful picture?" I remember how his expression changed and darkened when he realized I was asking him to do something different. He hated change.

But he knew what I wanted. He understood. I could tell.

Half an hour later, he came out of his bedroom with another map.

"No. This is not what I asked for. Come on, Zachary. Haven't you done enough maps?"

He looked at the floor and rolled his shoulders back and upward, just barely, but enough to show that he meant it as a gesture of defiance. His mouth was set in a taut line; his eyes were alight. I leaned forward until the tips of our noses were almost touching. "Now listen to me. I want you to go back to your room and I want you to draw me a picture of Mister Troiano's house. Or a car parked outside. Or a dog. I don't really care. Anything you can actually see. But not—absolutely *not*—another map. No. More. Maps. Understand?" And I crumpled the map he'd just given me into a ball and dropped it on the floor.

When he came out of his room, he brought me another map. It was the *same* map, in fact, but he'd drawn it in orange this time instead of purple.

And suddenly the weight of it all, of my entire stupid thwarted uphill life, was just too fucking much for me to carry, not even one more step.

Something inside me just broke.

I don't really remember the next moments clearly. I do remember reaching for the maps on his wall, grasping and clawing at them, ripping them down until there were none left, nothing left on the walls except random corners held fast by tape or pushpins.

I remember that I couldn't stop myself.

I remember that I didn't *want* to stop myself.

I remember whirling around, looking for something else to destroy as Zachary's fantastic atlas fluttered around me, in tatters and shreds on the floor. He stood in the doorway, watching me with that impassive look on his face, the one I'd come to know so well. But this time, there was something else behind his eyes, something I recognized right away: Defeat.

I'd seen it in my own face in the bathroom mirror, countless times. And now I'd put it on his as well.

What have I done?

I bent down and began gathering the pieces and fragments together into a pile, mostly because I didn't know what else to do. *I can fix this*, I was thinking, *of course I can, I can just tape them back together and he could put them back up where they had been and we could pretend that this never happened. All it would take was some tape and some time.*

I carried the pile into the kitchen. I remember my hands, so unsteady with adrenaline and shame. I started sliding the pieces around on the kitchen table, looking for the common seams, any ripped edges that fit together. I kept pulling too much tape out of the dispenser, and the overlong pieces twisted around and stuck to themselves. *Shorter pieces, idiot.* I couldn't find all the shreds of some of the maps. Through it all Zachary stood in the doorway, watching me as I tried to undo my mistake, his face still a blank mask.

A little tape and time can fix anything. And for a second—not *even* a second, really—I almost believed it myself.

On the plane, in the row next to mine there is a boy who looks like Zachary did the last time I saw him. He sits in the middle seat, sandwiched between his parents, who fiddle with various electronic devices and efficiently parry their son's tactics for drawing their attention. Soon he gives up and takes out a coloring book.

"He hasn't drawn anything for an entire week," I remember saying to Doctor Behrendt. "I don't remember the last time he went without drawing for that long."

"It's just an adjustment period."

"I really wish I hadn't done that. God, I feel horrible."

"He'll come around. Don't worry."

The parents of the boy each slip on their headphones and sequester themselves from the world around them. The boy continues with his task, shading around the negative spaces on the page, losing himself in his work, happy in his isolation.

●

Zachary was not in his bed when I went to wake him the following Tuesday morning. He was not in the house. He was not in the back yard. He was not on the stoop.

He was gone.

What I found instead was a roomful of brand new maps, hand-drawn in crayon and covering every square centimeter of wall space. In some spots they were tacked on three or four deep. Roads and rivers from one map abruptly connected with those on its neighbor. This pattern repeated over and over until they formed a vast, intricate multi-colored fractal of sharp turns and dead ends.

It was like a hallucinogenic snowflake of cartographic impossibility.

I froze, took it all in for a moment. These were not the maps I had taped back together. These were all new, every single one, exact copies of the one he had drawn for me that I crumpled up and tossed at his feet the other week.

It must have taken him days to draw them.

Or maybe he did it all in one night.

I looked closer. Where was this place supposed to be? I'd developed a talent for identifying the locations depicted in Zachary's always-unlabeled maps over the last year and a half. But I didn't recognize this one. There were elements that seemed familiar on their own, but taken together it was all just topographic gibberish.

The police came soon after. Officers spent most of the day swarming all through my house, taking photos and writing in notebooks and mostly ignoring me while I tried to explain things to an earnest young patrolman and a lean, middle-aged detective who mostly just asked the same questions the patrolman did. I watched one of the other cops carefully place Zachary's hairbrush into a plastic bag and take it out to his car. My neighbors lingered across the street and watched the chaos in silence.

It was just like on TV.

The detective asked a series of questions about Zachary's father: where he was, what was their relationship, would Zachary have tried to go there, things like that.

"Oh, I doubt Warren had anything to do with this," I told her. "He lacks the follow-through."

"Maybe not," the detective said. "But we have to check anyway."

"Really, you shouldn't bother. I'm certain he left on his own."

"And what makes you say that?" the detective asked.

I paused. The answer to that question wouldn't make any sense to someone like her. The answer was in the maps, the maps he left behind. He had clearly put a lot of effort into them. He wouldn't have bothered unless it was important. I had stared at them for nearly an hour that morning before something in the web of boundaries and conduits and colors jarred something loose in my brain, and I recognized this new atlas for what it was: a goodbye note.

No, wait. It was his itinerary, a puzzle left for me to decipher. A puzzle that, even after I solved it, would still tell me nothing.

No. It was both.

I didn't know *how* I knew that. I just did.

"Just a feeling I have," I said with a shrug instead. "A mother's intuition."

When they had all finally gone, I went out and sat down near the bottom of the steps and wrapped myself in my arms. A woman wearing a gray pantsuit and a bulbous red motorcycle helmet puttered by on a motorscooter. A man walking a golden retriever and reading something on his phone passed in the other direction.

The street, the city, went on with its day.

●

Warren lived in a treeless pasture a few miles east of Modesto. That's where he went after he moved out. At some point before that and without me knowing a thing about it, he had plopped down a pair of shipping containers, welded them together in the shape of a giant L, and put the whole thing up on pilings. Now he called it home. It took me three hours to drive there. I'd only been there once before: I had needed his signature on a sheaf of documents to finalize the divorce, and there was no way I was going to let him drag this out any longer than it had to be. I might have missed it completely if I hadn't spotted his old Saab parked in the driveway.

I was shocked that it still ran. But then I got closer and noticed the two flat tires and the spiderwebs between the mirror and the door.

The house, if that's what you'd call it, was also looking worse for wear since I'd last seen it. The east side had a noticeable slump to it—wind and drought had loosened the dirt beneath the pilings—and there were rust streaks running down from the windows and along the main center seam. The windows themselves were coated in a thin gray film.

It hardly looked like the command center for one of the most heavily trafficked conspiracy theory websites on the internet, the passion project Warren had somehow managed to turn into a steady source of income.

Then again, maybe that's *exactly* what it looked like.

This was the middle of nowhere. The nearest building was at least a mile away. Zachary could not have found his way out here. The fact that he never drew a Modesto map just confirmed that in my mind, though I didn't quite know why.

Those maps, every last one of them, sat on the passenger's seat, tucked away in an oversized messenger bag. I still wasn't sure this was the right thing; the last thing I wanted to do was offer Warren even the appearance of an invitation back into my life. I assumed he knew about Zachary's disappearance; he did not know about the maps, or about Zachary's years-long silence. But he was both Zachary's father and an authority—of sorts, anyway—on the unexplained and unexplainable. As dispiriting as it was, Warren was my best option.

I expected the interior of Warren's house to match the squalor of the exterior. But the inside was clean, almost minimalist. The walls were painted in a light cream color and filled with modular shelving units, each of which was filled with tidy rows of binders and deep plastic bins. Light flowed in through the large windows in the back. The door to the home's other room was shut, and a pair of women's boots rested between the front door and Warren's compact desk.

"I find it's easiest to keep on top of what's happening if I stay organized," he said, tracking my gaze. "I never could see the point of taping all your evidence to the wall and then doing that thing with the yarn. It looks distracting as hell."

He spread the contents of the atlas across the floor and perched himself on his orange Ikea couch like some kind of paranoid hipster gargoyle. He had lost weight since I'd last seen him and his beard had filled in.

Somehow those benign changes in his appearance combined to make him seem more alert, more amped. He rubbed his hands together, chewed lightly on the base of his thumb as he studied the maps before him.

"Could be tied to FEMA," he said after a minute or two. "They're into pretty much everything these days. You ever heard of the Incunabula Papers? Seems to fit—or—*oooh!*—the Denver airport."

I was almost afraid to ask. "What about the Denver airport?"

"Teleportation machines of some kind. Time travel—I mean, we don't know yet if it's a mechanical manipulation of the space-time continuum or if it's just some natural phenomenon the government stumbled onto by accident. But I have people in the field working on that."

One of the many mysteries of Warren has always been the question of just how much he really believed the crap he wrote. He was a smart man—I would not have married him otherwise—and I always thought there was a tongue-in-cheek aspect to his work on his website. But I was never certain of that, and now I felt my calculus shifting. "I don't think there is one of Denver in there, though," I said, gesturing at the maps. He shook his head vigorously.

"Well no, there wouldn't be, would there? Why would he need a map of Denver? It's just, like, a way station, just sitting there at the center of a massive hub-and-spoke system that reaches . . . well, we don't know yet just how far it goes. But it's pretty damn far, I can tell you that much. They might have fitted him with an RFID implant so they can track him whenever he goes . . . wherever it is he goes."

I began snatching the maps up off the floor and stuffing them back into my messenger bag. This visit was a mistake. "That doesn't make sense," I said. "Not at all."

"It makes perfect sense if you've done the work to understand it all, Julia," he said, squinting at me and rubbing his bald head. Still squatting there on the couch, he suddenly looked very much like a chimpanzee. "And no offense, but you just haven't done the work."

"There is no amount of work that could possibly make sense out of any of your gibberish," I snapped. Why had I ever thought coming here would be a good idea? Warren is toxic. Warren is a vortex. This result was inevitable. It had been from the moment I thought of it.

"I don't mean that," he said, shaking his head, slowly this time. "The fact that you even came here tells me you're more lost than you realize."

●

I arrive at my hotel in Lucca early in the evening. It is clean and modern, just inside the old city walls. The warmth of the day still lingers in my room. The walls are thin too: I can hear the couple next door, speaking in a language that sounds like Italian but isn't.

I open the window to let the room air out and move to the bed. There I unfold my own map. There is nothing mystical or mysterious about it: it's a standard Rand-McNally map of the world, the kind you can still get almost anywhere. Or at least, I assume you still can. I've had this one for years now.

If you could see this map, if you were here on this adventure with me right now, you might ask what the circles mean. That's my system. I circle a city in green when I arrive. If I see him during my visit, I fill in the circle with a red felt-tip.

Rotterdam is marked in red: that's where I saw him walking along the Lijnbaan. I filled in Quito's circle after I saw him getting on a bus there. Another time he was sketching the crowd in a market in Lvov. There was Halifax, Christchurch, a few other places. Seoul. He was in Seoul too, slurping down a late lunch in a noodle shop. That was the first time I saw him. I spotted him so easily that time, towering above the crowd as he did. He doesn't always look the same: sometimes he's older than he should be, sometimes younger. Other times he's right around the age he should be, which right now would be twenty.

This is my map of the map cities I've visited so far. My dream is to one day sit with him and show him this map, unfold it in front of him and show him all the places I went to find him, ask him if he saw me waving that time in New Orleans or Phnom Penh.

I want to hear about all the places he has been, the things he has seen, the adventures he's had.

I want to ask him why he never came home.

For now, I find Lucca on my map city map and circle it in green.

One step at a time.

●

I drove home from Warren's feeling foolish and angry the entire way. I was tired of people telling me I hadn't done the work. Warren. Doctor Behrendt. The grief pimps in my support group, Parents of the Disappeared, kept telling me this exact thing on the third Thursday of every month.

What about the posters I put up all over the city? What about the hours I spent doing research online? The reward—I'm the one who put that together. What about this limp and pointless support group? That's all work. Doesn't any of it count?

No. That stuff was nice, but it wasn't what they meant. I was dodging my grief, keeping myself busy and hiding behind those maps I wouldn't stop talking about, not doing the work of coming to terms with my loss.

Well, what did they know? They were nothing but a bunch of grandstanders, each trying outdo the others in displays of performative bereavement. I considered making scorecards, like in the Olympics, and holding them up at the end of our share sessions.

"Those maps aren't going to help you get better," they told me the night I decided to leave and never come back. "They're a security blanket. Help is only going to come from inside yourself."

More platitudes.

"And you are confident that was the correct decision?" Doctor Behrendt asked me the following week.

"Yes." He waited for more, but that was all I was going to give him. Anything else would have been superfluous.

"And why is that?" he prodded.

I shrugged. "They just . . . didn't *get* it, I guess. I explained it to them, probably a dozen times. About how he was with the maps. It didn't mean anything to them. They didn't want to hear it."

"Or perhaps it was you who did not wish to hear."

"Oh, come on. Not you too."

"It has been months," he said. "Your progress is slower than it should be. You must do the work to get better. I believe the maps inhibit you from doing so."

"The maps *are* the work," I countered. "Besides, you're the one who said they were a form of communication. You said that."

"The maps are a red herring. I was wrong about them. There is no message for you to find in them." He took off his glasses and looked out the window. "I am afraid I must recommend that you destroy them."

Was this a metaphor for something? I waited for him to continue. But he didn't, and I realized it was not a metaphor at all: he meant for me to go home and literally set a match to the last and most important thing I still had of Zachary.

"I don't think I can do that," I said. "And I don't know how you can think I could do that, after all this time."

He stood and went to his desk. "I know it is difficult to contemplate such an act. But I fear our sessions will not be productive until you do. So please consider it." He looked down at his desk calendar. "Our next session is scheduled for two weeks from tomorrow. Until then, think about what I have said."

"I'll think about it, I promise," I said as I stood up and shouldered my bag, relieved to finally be done with therapy forever.

●

Of course I didn't burn the maps. I would never find him without them. There was nothing more obvious in the world.

It was the first time in my life that I ever ignored doctor's orders.

I don't know where I would be now if I had obeyed. But I would not be here, sipping coffee in this café, in the old Roman Amphitheater. The whole place is a tourist trap now, the crumbling walls ringed with carts and stalls, restaurants and cafés retrofitted into the cavernous cellarlike spaces along the bottom. But it's still beautiful. Warm, though; I probably should have chosen someplace on the other side of the amphitheater instead. I don't like the sun all that much. In all these years of traveling, I've never really acclimated to it.

When I see him, it happens so quickly that I almost miss it.

It's just a glimpse, really—not much more than a flash before he ducks back into one of the shops about halfway between me and the amphitheater entrance—but it's enough. He looks to be about his right age this time.

I take another sip of coffee, close my guidebook and put it in my bag, and wait for him to come out of the shop again. My heart quickens, as it always does when I catch sight of him.

I'm not going to let him disappear on me again. Not this time.

I crane my neck and spot him again, by the postcard rack. Buying something, it looks like.

He turns and moves off, toward the opposite end of the amphitheater. I follow. I try to keep a comfortable distance between us so he doesn't notice me. He ducks out through the exit on the amphitheater's shady side. I try to keep up, weaving between the thicket of tourists, but I lose sight of him as he emerges from the darkness of the tunnel and disappears into the bright sunshine outside.

I flip a coin in my head: left. *There he is.* How did he get so far ahead of me? He turns down an alley and I have to break into a jog to close the distance before he slips away again.

I round the corner of the same alley and stop. Empty. Also, it's a dead end. There are five or six shops, but only one of them, a gelateria, is open.

He *must* have gone in there. There's no other possibility.

God, I'm so close now. After all this time. I can *feel* it. My heart flutters into my throat and I step inside the shop.

But it is also empty, deserted except for the elderly proprietor behind the counter.

Empty.

How is it empty? *Where the fuck did he go?* I want to scream, to cry, to smash things in a rage.

I take a deep breath and collect myself.

"Excuse me, sir," I say to the old man. My Italian is rudimentary at best, but I know enough to make myself understood, more or less. "I am looking for a young man. I think he came in here. Have you seen him?"

I describe him; the man just shrugs and goes back to his copy of *Corriere dello Sport*. He ignores me for several seconds before I get the message: as far as he is concerned, our conversation is over.

Maybe I got it wrong. Maybe he went down a different street.

Or maybe he just disappeared the moment I lost sight of him.

Maybe it's wormholes, like Warren said all those years ago. Shortcuts through time and space that reroute through the Denver airport, or whatever it was.

Could I follow him through a wormhole?

Would I even recognize one if I saw it?

Goddammit.

I drop into one of the rickety wooden chairs. The elderly man glares at me. Who gives a shit. I ignore him. I am suddenly very tired. All the years of traveling, all these joyless miles carrying the weight of my hopes and expectations—now I feel every second, every step.

So close. I was so damn close.

I could always try again. There are more maps, so many more maps. But just the idea of picking another random map from the pile and traveling there, with no guarantees, just sinks me, like a millstone around the neck.

I can't keep doing this to myself. I just can't.

I wonder if it's too late to start doing the work.

But I've *been* working. Remembering is so much harder than forgetting.

It's time to go home.

I stand up to leave, to begin the journey back to San Francisco. I know that once I get back there, I may never leave again.

Then: the muffled sound of a toilet flushing behind a closed door. The rushing of an open faucet.

The bathroom.

I look over at the man behind the counter, my eyebrows raised in silent inquiry. But he has gone back to his paper, to ignoring me.

This is it.

I close my eyes, take a deep breath and hold it in. *One way or another, this is it.*

The bathroom door swings open with a loud creak.

I open my eyes as wide as they'll go.

Controlled Descent

Time: 1917 hours
Altitude: 34,100 ft
Speed: 480 mph
Position: Somewhere over Nebraska

Cynthia would do bodily harm to a stranger for an ice-cold Coke just now—not that her joints would allow such a thing—but no matter how many times she pushes the call button, no stewardesses ever come. Wait, that ain't right. Flight attendants. That's what they are now. *The world changes so dang fast these days,* she thinks, then tries to remember the last time she flew on an airplane. Probably that time when she and Glenn went down to Florida, and he's been gone since . . . well, all right, call it twenty-five years then.

She shifts her legs in the tiny space in front of her. "I know I haven't flown in a long while," she says to no one in particular, "but did airplanes always used to be so dang *cramped?*"

Nobody pays her the slightest attention. Somewhere over Iowa, the 777 shuttling them from Columbus to Sacramento turned into a party plane. Even though the seatbelt lights have been on for the entire flight, people are getting out of their seats, talking to and laughing with complete strangers, their relief and elation bubbling up and out of them in an endless froth of chitchat.

"What about you?" someone says to Cynthia. A man, standing in the aisle by her row, looks at her expectantly. He has a receding hairline and a potato-shaped face and wears the kind of grin that Cynthia has always associated with simple-mindedness. "Ever been to California before?"

California—they got a different name for that now too. Western Autonomous Region. The Fox News people like to call it by its initials: the WAR. That's where she's going. Off to the WAR.

"I never have," she says. "Never had the urge to go. Still don't, not that anyone asked me."

Melanie, in the seat in front of her, turns around. "That's not true, Mother. We talked about this plenty of times."

"It most certainly *is* true. Did you ask before you put our names into that website? Did you ask me if I *wanted* to uproot myself and drag my life clear across the country? Leave my home? You did not."

Potato-face clears his throat. "I'm just going to . . ." he says, trailing off and pointing toward his seat up toward the front. "Yeah."

"I know there's nothing to be done about it now," she continues, ignoring the simpleton's departure. She closes her eyes, fans herself with her hand.

"Mother, are you all right?" Melanie asks.

"Just a little light-headed is all. Nothing a Coke wouldn't fix right up, if I could even *get* one," she says, and she presses the call button once more.

Time: 2043 hours
Altitude: 33,000 ft
Speed: 496mph
Position: Just east of Salt Lake City, Utah

Melanie swallows two more of those pills Doctor Weller prescribed for her a couple months back. In the seat next to her, Danny gives her the stink-eye. She doesn't have any water to wash them down—what is going *on* with the flight attendants, anyway?—and she's not supposed to be taking them anymore. But she has talked herself into the notion that these are special circumstances, that she needs something to keep this whole thing from unraveling on her, right here on the plane. Just like the whole country has been for the last several years: pulling itself apart, cooking itself down to slag for no reason other than simple spite.

She closes her eyes and takes a deep breath. Right away she feels the tension melting away, and even though she can't quite shut her mind of the unnerving libretto of the New America—frantic rallies of young berserkers in white polos, screaming bile and hate; or the "Whites Only" signs that seemed to sprout up everywhere at once; or those terrifying slack-jawed baby goons patrolling the streets in their trucks, caressing their guns and threatening you with their dead-eyed stares; or that bomb they found at the newspaper offices down in Dayton—even with all that, she is more relaxed than she's been in weeks.

She listens to Cynthia behind her, complaining to her neighbor about how her own daughter tricked her into leaving the house her dear departed husband built for her, how this whole thing was just a silly overreaction, and boy wouldn't they feel dumb in a few months when they all came crawling back home. *Fruits and nuts,* she's saying now. *That's what they got in California. Or should I say,* Mexi-*fornia. Whole place is full of crazy people. Nuts. Liberal left-wing raving moonbats. Always has been. And when I say fruits, I'm talking about—*

Melanie slips her earbuds in and turns on some music. There was a time once when she would have interrupted her mother, apologized for her, but those days are long gone. She's already done more than her share to save Cynthia from herself. It's true that she didn't say anything when she registered the five of them for the relocation lottery on the first day it opened, but considering the long odds, she didn't really see the point. Later, she heard on the news that in just the first two days, over three million people requested official permission to dislocate themselves and cart whatever they could carry with them to WAR, where the country would finally make its metaphorical left-right divide into something real: Liberals on one side of the line, conservatives on the other, once and for all.

The website crashed every few minutes from all the traffic. But she kept trying, and a month later, she got a letter from the Department of the Interior, the agency in charge of the Partition Program. *Partition.* Like what they did in India back in the 1940s, when the Muslims and the Hindus couldn't get along, couldn't live in the same country with each other, and the only solution was to separate the two, like cranky children on a long car trip, and invent Pakistan for all the Muslims to go live in.

Melanie wasn't sure how she knew about this; she might have seen a movie about it once. The whole idea seemed silly to her, that drawing a new line on a map and moving some people around could really solve anything.

But you never know. Maybe it'll work better this time. This is America, after all.

She gulped down a lungful of air. Ripped open the envelope. Read the words *Your family has been selected.* There it was. They were going to the west coast. *I did it,* she thought. *I saved the family.*

That's what her mother doesn't understand. What she'll *never* understand. She did this for *her*. For her and Danny and Cody and Laura.

The sounds of laughter and revelry seep around Melanie's earbuds and into her consciousness, pulling her back from the brink of sleep. People are dancing in the aisles now, yell-singing songs about California into each other's faces. It's a certified party.

She smiles. *It's almost right in front of us now,* she thinks, and for just an instant she pictures them all living in a tidy and stylish ranch house on a cul-de-sac, grapefruit trees in the front yard and a mountain range in the back, the entire landscape awash in sunshine like an overexposed photograph before she realizes that the house in her vision is the one from *The Brady Bunch.* She rests her hand on Danny's bicep and her head on his shoulder.

"You okay, babe?" he asks.

"I think it's the pills," she says. "They've never hit me this hard before."

Time: 2201 hours
Altitude: 26,650 ft
Speed: 471mph
Position: North of Sacramento, California, WAR

The seatback monitor in front of Cynthia is showing her footage from the latest uprising in the northeast, in Worcester, Massachusetts: Eighteen dead, three of them police officers. She watches a phalanx of cops in riot gear huddling behind their man-sized Plexiglass shields and shooting gas canisters into the throng of agitators. Thick yellow clouds sweep across the crowd, which shows no inclination to disperse. Cars smolder and smoke in the background.

Annoyed, she switches it off; the monitor defaults to the interactive flight map. *They shouldn't show that sort of thing on an airplane,* she thinks. Likely to get people all riled up. But the cabin is calm and quiet now: she can make out a soft-voiced conversation here and there, but it seems like most people are napping now. She's not surprised. Things were getting pretty raucous there for a while. But eventually folks just partied themselves out.

She contemplates the interactive map in front of her. A little animated airplane slowly ticks off the last few millimeters of a thin red arc stretching from Columbus to Sacramento. *Finally.* Just about there now. It's been a long flight, and her knees are starting to ache. Outside and below, a filigree of tiny lights crisscrosses the terrain and rolls off into the distance. Cynthia presses her forehead to the window. She has never seen a city like this before, the lights from so high up. To her mind, cities at night have always been something to avoid, places of danger and vitiation. But from up here, it's peaceful, mesmerizing.

What would Glenn think of this, she wonders, but only for a moment. She knows exactly what he would think: that this entire chicken-shit scheme was half-baked from the start. He was not a man to tolerate foolishness or quitting, and he no doubt would have considered the entire idea of a Western Autonomous Region to be both of those things. A safe space for precious little snowflakes too weak to fight for what they claimed to value. No place for *his* family, that's for damn sure.

No, that place was—*is*—the house he built for her, almost fifty years ago. It took him the better part of a year. He built it as a surprise, a gift for her, and even all these years later she still remembers the day he first brought her there so vividly: It was a raw, gray morning, and she wore a cream-colored crocheted scarf with matching hat and gloves. She remembers the wet leaves stuck in the windshield wipers of Glenn's turquoise Ford Fairlane, the faint smell of the stale cigarette butts in the ashtray, the Conway Twitty song playing softly on the radio. She remembers the unpaved driveway, how the mud tried to hold her shoes as she stepped out of the car. She remembers how it felt when she realized what was happening, how her breath caught and she couldn't quite get any coherent words out for a minute; it was like every Christmas and every birthday surprise she'd ever had, all rolled into one.

They had thirty-two happy years in that house. When he died, he died suddenly, and Cynthia didn't speak a word to anyone for nearly three full weeks. Melanie thought she might have had a small stroke herself; she had never known her mother to stay quiet for very long. Cynthia spent those three weeks sitting in Glenn's favorite recliner, watching one of the cable news channels. They were supposed to be living in the future now, but nobody ever told her that in the future, the world would be on fire. She usually watched with the sound off; she could usually get the gist of things just from the pictures and captions. And that gist was, things were different now. Things were different and they'd never go back to how they used to be, not ever again.

I never wanted to leave it, she thinks. *But I couldn't let them go without me. You understand that, don't you?*

She looks at the map again, drags her finger along the arc eastward, back to Ohio. Wishes it was just as simple as that.

Just as her finger reaches Columbus, the screen goes black.

She cranes her neck and looks across her row, at the seat backs on the rows in front of her. All the map screens are black now. *Must be about to land,* she thinks.

But the plane holds its course and altitude. Below them, the lights of Sacramento gradually thin out, eventually ceding the entire territory to the spreading darkness.

"What's happening?" she asks, of nobody in particular. "Why aren't we landing? Where are you taking us?" But there is no one to answer her.

Something is wrong. She knows it. But she can't quite *see* it; she can barely hold her thoughts in her mind for more than a few seconds before they slip away. *If only I wasn't so goddamn light-headed*, she thinks just before she passes out. *If only I could have got that Coke.*

Time: 2244 hours
Altitude: 13,200 ft and dropping
Speed: 525mph
Position: Over the Pacific Ocean

The innately terrifying sensation of freefall snaps Melanie awake. She blinks a few times, trying to flush the fog from her mind. Her family sleeps in the seats around her: Danny, snoring as usual; Cynthia in the row behind them, her head lolling with every nudge of turbulence; Cody and Laura curled together in the row in front of her.

Outside, she sees the glint of the full moon reflected from below. It is a bright night, and she can see the surface gently ripple and swell. It takes her a moment to realize that they are over water, and that they are descending rapidly.

The cabin is silent. She is the only one awake.

What the hell is going on?

But she knows. Even before she finishes the thought, she knows the answer. It's why there weren't any flight attendants.

She wonders what happens to an aircraft cabin that's been pumped full of almost-pure oxygen for five hours when it hits the surface at several hundred miles per hour.

She wonders why she didn't just let Cynthia stay in Ohio like she'd wanted. She had been ready to do it at one point, when Cynthia was at her most recalcitrant. *I can't force her to go against her will,* Melanie remembers telling Danny. But she couldn't let Cynthia be the anchor that bound them all to a sinking ship. She would cut her mother loose if she insisted on sabotaging the rest of them, and then bear that cross for the rest of her life.

And then the next day, Cynthia relieved her of that obligation. Melanie was grateful for that, as well as a little surprised that it wasn't shame she felt for having so seriously considered such a strict and pragmatic act of self-preservation, but rather pride.

Now look at us. I've doomed us all.

She wonders if she should wake her family up to say goodbye. This is her last chance to tell them all how much she loves them.

On the other hand, letting them skip the terrible knowledge of their own impending deaths seems like the best way to show them that love.

Not knowing what else to do, she tucks herself into the crash position and waits.

This isn't a very dignified way to go, she thinks, *but at least no one's here to see it.*

Time: 2245 hours

Altitude: 0 ft

Speed: 540mph

Position: In the Pacific Ocean

As the plane slams into the water and rips itself apart in the horrible anarchy of force and flame, Cynthia dreams, as she often does, of the house Glenn built for her almost fifty years ago. In the dream, Glenn is still alive. They are in bed asleep when a loud bang rattles and shakes the house to its foundation. *Oh my God, I think a truck hit the house*, she tells Glenn. He kisses her on the forehead and gets out of bed.

I'll take care of it, he says, and he opens the bedroom door and lets the water come rushing in.

It's so cold, she tells him. *Why's it so cold?*

Don't you worry about any of that, he says. *Just go back to sleep.*

I don't like it, she says. *Make it stop.*

It'll stop in a minute, he says as he climbs back into the bed with her. *But you just got to trust me.*

All right, she says. *I trust you*, and she feels the warmth of his body and the surety of his arms around her as the water takes them both.

Headbangers' Ball

Say what you will about the devil, but I have to hand it to him: Beelzebub knows how to stock a record store *right*. The one at the mall had newer stuff, was twice the size, and had a modern ventilation system that kept it from smelling like sour armpit and stale farts, but the devil was aiming for more of a niche market. Limited pressings from Denmark and Finland by bands whose names I couldn't even begin to pronounce. Framed collectibles and rarities covering almost every square inch of the faux-wood rec-room paneling. How much for that one? we'd ask and point. How much?

Every time, the devil craned his neck around slowly to look at whatever we'd just expressed an interest in, giving it the critical eyeballing of an experienced appraiser before turning back to face but not quite look at us. Then he'd quote us some ridiculous amount, which made no sense because nobody who had that kind of money to drop on signed publicity stills or framed backstage passes from Pink Floyd's last-ever show would even *think* to look for those things in a dump like this. And of course, it was the one thing in the whole store that didn't even *have* a price that had Clay's undivided attention from day one: that Kiss poster pinned up directly behind the register. It was the one that came with their *Unmasked* album, which we both agreed was their worst record to date, even worse than *Dynasty*, so if you could get the poster without having to buy the album you'd actually be coming out ahead. The poster was a stylized cartoon that showed all four band members removing full-face, harlequin-style masks, only to reveal that their actual faces are identical to the masks that had hidden them; they were, and always had been, exactly the freaks they appeared to be. What you see is what you get. The devil had ruined it by poking thumbtacks through the corners, and who knows how many years of smoke exposure had tinged the once-crisp whites a sickly yellow. But it was autographed by all four original band members, in fat silver Sharpie, and in my book that more than made up for the damage.

How much for the Kiss poster, Clay would ask every single time we were in there.

I'll never let that one go, the devil would say between drags, peering at us over his wire-rimmed glasses. Collector's item. Can't get those anymore.

Well, you can if you conjure it. And we knew he could, because we once saw him conjure up six breakfast burritos, right in front of us. One minute there's nothing on the counter, and then poof, a crisp white bag of tortillas and eggs, steam and grease.

I had my back turned, but Clay—my only friend and fellow untouchable in our high school's heartless caste system—swore by it. He had grown up churched but now only wore black t-shirts emblazoned with umlauts. Clay *knew* things. He knew about the ancient astronauts and time travel and what really happened to Atlantis. He knew the best ways to sober up quick before going home after a keg party. He knew how to make even the meanest junkyard dog lie down in front of you and lick your feet. He knew the best place to hit a guy if you wanted him to hit the floor fast, and the right way to touch a girl if you wanted her to forget the promises she made to herself.

Trust me, he said later. This all makes perfect sense. The best disguise is one nobody expects. The devil knows that better'n anyone.

I shrugged. *So I guess this is what we're doing this summer*, I thought. Another inside joke in the making, another hilarious story to tell each other next year while we pass his father's vodka bottle back and forth, a story that gets bigger and funnier with each retelling, even though we both know the truth of it. Sure, why not. What else was there to do?

●

It was a couple of weeks after we first found Joe Devil's place that Clay started to dig his hole in the back yard.

He'd wait to do his work until the sun was soft and low in the sky and the air was thick with moisture, when there was never any wind. He'd work without a shirt and I'd see the muscles in his back and shoulders constrict and extend, pulling and relaxing in tandem as he planted the shovel, over and over.

I did not have muscles like that. Maybe I should dig my own hole, I thought more than once. My house didn't have a big back yard like Clay's, and I wondered if my parents might finally notice something I did if I carved out a giant open pit right next to the front door.

Evenings were for digging, but our days were mostly occupied with robbing the devil blind. The way our little scam worked was this: Clay would distract him at the counter by pretending to want to sell him a stack of worthless records while I'd pluck albums out of the bins and peel off the price tags, which was easy enough because he used the cheap kind, without much glue on the back. Then we would sell his own stock back to him.

Check these out, Clay would say, positioning himself between me and the devil.

Every time, the same routine. Pass, the devil would say as he flipped each record aside, the word not spoken so much as simply allowed to fall out of his mouth and plonk onto the counter.

What? Seriously? Dude, it's in mint condition. Look at the jacket. The corners are still pointy.

Dude. (exhale, smoke) It's a fucking Debbie Boone record, and it's warped. Pass.

The smoke. He was always smoking something, either menthols or something else, something sweeter and heavier. The smoke swirling around him made the stool he was perched on look like it was teetering on the edge of a fissure to hell, a crack in the earth through which we could see the demons and damned at the center of the world, if only we could get around that counter.

You always bring me better stuff than your friend, the devil would say to me. I'll give you . . . eight and a quarter for the lot.

That's how he always talked. Eight and a quarter. Five and two quarters. Seven and a dime, a nickel and three Indian-head pennies. It's how we knew he wasn't what he pretended to be. Normal people with nothing to hide don't talk like that.

Sometimes we kept the records we stole from him, but usually we didn't. We would almost always take whatever cash he offered us. In that way, the devil ended up buying most of our cigarettes that summer.

●

Just like every summer, it was too hot to go outside much. The Florida sun blazed down and baked the blacktop parking lots until the heat radiated upwards and made the soles of your shoes sticky, and there was no shelter from it, no trees big enough or old enough to offer a couple of weary and shiftless teenagers any shade because they'd all been ripped out and replaced by saplings when the subdivisions went in. Then all the saplings died because they hadn't been planted properly in the first place. Some days we didn't want to walk the three miles round trip to the store, so we spent those afternoons in the garage, rearranging the letters in the store name—Melodie Music, that's what the devil called his store, couldn't even spell his own sign right—searching for cryptographic clues to the devil's origin. The most promising thing we found was "Die Scum I'm Leo."

Some nights we would sit out there by the hole, on the pile of dirt Clay built next to it, and smoke until his father came home. If you boys don't quit that smoking out there, he would call from the back porch, I will come out there and kick both your asses and *bury* y'all in that got-damn hole.

Sure, Dad, Clay would say under his breath, rolling his eyes and taking another drag. Whatever you say.

He'd been digging that hole in the back yard for three solid weeks before he finally answered when I asked him what it was for.

It's for Joe Devil, he said. So he can go back where he came from.

Gonna have to be a little deeper than that, I said.

Clay put down his shovel. Listen, he said. I have an idea. Tonight, like really late, you and me are gonna sneak out, head up to Joe Devil's, and have a look around.

Break in? I said. No fucking way. *Hell* no.

We have to, he said. It's the only way to know what we're really dealing with.

What, do you think he sleeps in there? In a coffin in the back room or something?

Well I've never seen any car in that parking lot of his, he said. So maybe, yeah. He might could be doing exactly that.

Or maybe he takes the bus, I said.

Just be ready when I get there, he said. And bring something heavy.

I think he's starting to get in your head, I told him.

Clay sucked hard on his cigarette. It withered down almost the whole way to the filter, and he flicked it away with a casual snap of his fingers. Probably, he said. Then he shrugged and said, too late to worry about that now, I guess. He's the devil. That's what he does.

●

That night I skipped dinner and watched *Jeopardy* instead. I was too nervous to eat and too distracted to even notice when the show ended until I was eleven minutes into *Wheel of Fortune*. Which I hated.

I kept rolling it over in my mind and coming back to the same conclusion. Clay was going too far. Stealing from the devil was one thing. But this, stepping into the devil's own lair and sneaking a look behind the curtain, intruding like that? It'd be *insulting* to him if we went through with this. Mocking him. There's no *way* that could possibly stand.

I knew I had to draw the line. Right here. Tonight. I had to tell him, Clay, you're getting a little weird lately, with this Joe Devil obsession and now this giant crater or burial pit or whatever it is you're digging in your back yard, I mean who does that, and you know, maybe instead of breaking into a record store tonight, we should just stay home and play Nintendo. Might be just what you need, brother.

I knew it was up to me to put a stop to this madness. I also knew I wouldn't.

Clay showed up around 12:15. I heard him snap his fingers, which was our prearranged signal, so I popped out the screen and hoisted myself through my bedroom window, dropping soundlessly behind the cluster of sabal palms.

Like a goddamn ninja, he said. His backpack sagged like a full diaper and he kept tugging on the straps and rolling his shoulders. He was smiling. Taking action—*any* action, and with Clay, the more ill-conceived the better— was usually all it took to put him in a better mood.

Sorry I took so long, he said. I wanted to be here at 11:58.

I looked at him, not understanding.

You know, like the Iron Maiden song? he said. Two minutes to midnight?

Yeah, sure. What's in the backpack?

You'll see when we get there, he said. His expression darkened. Where's yours?

I couldn't get anything out of the garage, I said. My dad keeps track of that stuff.

He sighed. Jesus Christ, you big pussy. We're not gonna be gone all night. You'da had it back before he even knew it was gone.

We walked the whole way in silence. The muscles in my arms trembled, and I couldn't tell if it was from the midnight chill or the anticipation of what was coming, of finally knowing the unknowable.

Watch for cops, Clay whispered back at me after a while. And run if you see any.

A few minutes later we stood at the back door to Melodie Music. It was tucked behind the dumpster, far from the glare of the streetlights and hidden like a secret doorway cut into the side of some ethereal mountain, beyond which lies only doom in the form of some kind of cursed and irresistible treasure. Only instead of runes, it bore a tiny NO TRESPASSING sign in silver and red. Clay removed his backpack, set it down on the ground, and fished around inside for a minute. When he stood up again, he held in his hands a jet-black bowling ball.

It was the heaviest thing I could find, he said. Besides, my dad'll never miss it. He hasn't bowled since before Mom left, I think.

And before I could decide whether to laugh at the absurdity or protest the inevitable, he hefted that fifteen-pound orb back and up and straight down again, smashing the door handle with a fat crunch. My heart fluttered, and for just a moment I couldn't breathe. This was *happening*.

The door handle was made of tougher stuff than it first appeared; it took Clay two more strikes to knock it completely loose. He looked over at me.

You ready for this? he asked.

I said nothing, even though I was quite certain I was not in fact ready for this. Whatever *this* was. He smiled, and his eyebrow arched up.

Too late now, he said, and pulled the door open, and we were inside. There was no going back.

I gulped down a frantic breath and held it, half-convinced that it would be my last. I expected to spontaneously combust any second now. The store's trademark scent, somewhere between musty and rancid, was even more pungent at night, probably because the air conditioner was off. Clay produced a flashlight from his backpack and switched it on. The place was even more of a shithole than I had realized: Cardboard boxes full of unsellable Pablo Cruise and Shaun Cassidy records stacked ceiling-high in some places. Empty cigarette packs. Crumpled paper bags that had conveyed countless high-carb, high-fat fast food breakfasts and lunches from all the local deep-fryers straight to Joe Devil's unappeasable gut. Illegible hand-scrawled invoices and receipts. Yellowing and curling old photos pinned to the corkboard, pictures of Joe with Ritchie Blackmore and Frank Zappa and, improbably enough, Kenny Rogers.

Here we go, Clay said. If he's here, we'll find him.

It was only then that I noticed he was holding a machete.

Holy *fuck*! Where did that come from?

Backpack, he said. Found it in the garage. Spent like an hour sharpening it before I came over.

Clay. Come on, man. Why would you bring *that*? What could you possibly need that for?

Because, he said, if the devil's here, I'm going to take his fucking head and I'm going to bury it in my back yard.

I wasn't sure he'd be able to sever much of anything with that blade, no matter how sharp it was—it looked too flimsy to me, almost like a Fisher-Price version of the real thing—but I wasn't up for putting my suspicions to the test.

You can't possibly be serious, I said.

Serious as a heart attack, son.

Dude. He's not here. We've been through the whole place.

You give up too easy, he said. You always do. There's a trap door somewhere. Bet you anything.

What if there is, I said. How the hell are you gonna find it in this fucking mess?

Guess I'll start here, he said, and he yanked down one of the stacks of record boxes. I jumped out of the way as they crashed down in front of me, their contents spilling out and clattering across the dingy linoleum.

Nope, he said. No trap door there. Might be something behind this bulletin board though.

Jesus, dude. You're gonna trip the alarm.

There's no fucking alarm in here, Clay said. I mean, just look at this place. Huh—I thought for sure there'd be a control panel or something there, he added, and he smashed the corkboard against the desk again and again until it broke in half. Pushpins flew in every direction, and all the photos documenting Joe's fleeting brushes with fame fluttered to the floor.

Well shit, he said. Help me move that filing cabinet.

No, I said.

It'll be fun, he said, which is what he always said to get me to do something that would obviously be anything but. You'll see.

No, dude. This is . . . this is too much. You're taking this way too fucking far.

We are talking about the devil, my friend, he said. I know you didn't come up in any church so you might not know this. But when it comes to the devil, there is no such thing as too far.

Holy shit. My old-school Polish Catholic, four-masses-a-week grandmother didn't even believe in Satan as a walking, talking entity. But Clay did, and even as well as I knew him, I never would have guessed it.

Clay, man, this guy isn't the devil, I said. All we're doing here is bullying the fat kid.

If you wanna leave, don't let me keep you. He gave the massive filing cabinet along the far wall of the office an exploratory shove. It didn't budge. But I got shit left to do here.

Okay then, I said. I guess I'll see you tomorrow?

Sure, he said. No hard feelings.

I was relieved to be excused from whatever this had turned into, and simultaneously ashamed of my relief at leaving my only friend to face his unnameable demons alone. But I couldn't be part of that. I walked home quickly, keeping to the shadows, and I was back in my bed by a little past 2 a.m.

●

I slept poorly that night, tossing and turning in that shallow space between consciousness and dreams where the two overlap and take pot shots at each other. My guilt was keeping me awake, and in the morning I resolved to walk up to Joe Devil's place that day—on my own; Clay wasn't invited—and actually spend some money there. It was a half-measure, if even that, but it was all I could think of to do. I decided to consider it a first step toward redemption and see where it led me.

The sweltering air outside was almost too thick to breathe, and it was barely eleven in the morning. The walk felt uphill. I was dreading my arrival, where I'd have to account to myself for what we'd done the night before without giving myself—or Clay—away. I was not confident I had that kind of deception in me, at least not that morning.

When I got to the store, Joe Devil was camped behind the register as usual, busied with some of the inscrutable paperwork that I always assumed just came with adulthood. He did not notice me come in, but I noticed a 33-inch-by-22-inch empty space on the wall behind him that had not been there before.

You sold the Kiss poster, I said. *Shit*. I hadn't meant to blurt that out like that.

Joe's head snapped up and, upon seeing me, his eyes narrowed to serpentine slits.

I didn't *sell* it, he hissed. Someone *stole* it.

I just stood there. I was aware my mouth was open. I desperately hoped that nothing would come out of it.

Broke in last night and just yanked it down off, he went on. Trashed the back room too, looking for money or drugs or who even knows. Probably that friend of yours, now that I think of it.

Couldn't be, I said. Why would you think it was him? I was *this* close to saying *Clay* instead of *him*, and congratulated myself for not completely ruining everything in the first thirty seconds.

He sighed, took off his glasses and rubbed his eyes, and for the first time I saw him in the light, saw him for what he was: a beaten, fat old man in a Goodwill sweater who couldn't even control what happened in his own store, let alone the underworld. I had never seen him look less powerful than he did just then.

Cut the shit, kid. You and your little buddy have been robbing me blind. I don't know how, but it's gotta be you. The books don't balance. Nothing adds up right. I know it ain't me, and nobody else is in here all the goddamn time like you two are.

Now if you don't mind, he went on, I have these police reports to fill out.

I was frozen where I stood, right in front of New Releases. He had seen right through us, and he didn't even need the powers of darkness to do it.

Redemption was going to take a little more work than I'd thought.

I flipped through the bin behind me until I found something that looked like it might have the potential to be interesting—something by Zodiac Mindwarp, I don't remember the title—and, head down like a condemned man petitioning for clemency from the gallows, brought it to the register and set it on the counter. I fished a ten dollar-bill out of my pocket and placed it on top of the record.

Joe Devil eyeballed me like he was sizing me up for a fight. Then he put the record back behind the counter and shoved my cash into his pocket. Now get the fuck out, he growled, and don't ever come back.

•

I actually saw the Kiss poster once more after that, or at least, I saw a corner of it. It was in the hole in Clay's back yard, already under a few shovels' worth of backfill. Clay was standing at the lip of the crater, shovel balanced on one shoulder and cigarette in his other hand, when I got to his house that afternoon. He looked like he'd been waiting for me to show up.

I may not have got him, he said. Clay's words came slowly and evenly, and his posture looked loose and languid; he was calmer than I'd seen him in weeks. But I got his talisman.

He can't stay here now, he added, and he pitched another shovelful of dirt back into the hole. He has to leave.

He knows it was you, I said. He was filling out police reports.

It doesn't matter, he said. He has no power without that. That's why he'd never sell it to me.

What you see is what you get, I thought. Joe Devil was never anything but exactly what he appeared to be. There was nothing of him to unmask.

Dude, he never had any power in the first place. He's just some guy.

Clay paused mid-shovel and looked off into the distance. He is *now*, anyway, he said, and then the poster vanished for good, along with Clay's own mask, beneath three or four pounds of dust and clay.

The surprising thing is that Clay turned out to be right. Less than three weeks later, Joe Devil was gone, vanished completely, without fanfare or even a "going out of business" sale. Melodie Music was replaced by a sewing supply shop by the middle of October, and that was that. You'd never have known he'd been there at all.

Clay and I never spoke of Joe Devil after that. Plenty of afternoons and evenings, we would sit in a pair of cheap green plastic chairs and smoke cigarettes just a foot or two away from that filled-in hole and pretend that none of it had ever happened. For Clay, there just wasn't any point in doing otherwise. It was a closed subject, and there would be nothing to gain from rehashing any of it.

Eventually, the grass reclaimed that patch of freshly turned earth, and the exact site of the poster's interment was forgotten. I moved on to other things. I ended up needing redemption for some of them, too.

FANCY GAP

There is a place in Virginia where you can drive south and north at the same time. It's right where two interstates cross, cutting through swaths of butternut and red cedar like baby's first X. For about seven miles the two numbers share the same asphalt, and which direction you're going depends solely on which highway you think you're on.

If you think about this for a minute, it will make sense. Draw yourself a map if you need help.

This only works because the asphalt isn't pointing either south or north. It runs east to west, so when you are on this particular stretch of road you are actually traveling in *three* directions at once: north, south and either into or away from the mountain sunrise, as it chases away the last slippery tendrils of low-lying morning fog.

With interstate highways, the long run is what's important. In the long run, we are all wherever we are supposed to be. In the long run, we are all dead.

Which way you headed? you could call out to drivers passing the other way. *South*, they'd answer. *Me too!* you'd shout back. And then you'd continue along in opposite directions.

Or you could change directions with nothing more than a thought. One moment, you're heading north to Roanoke, but then it hits you that you don't want nothing to do with her anymore so instead you're driving south, toward Charlotte. You just change which number you're on.

And you don't even have to move the steering wheel to do it, because sometimes, not often but sometimes, life is just as easy as you always wished it was.

Fight or Flight

From the moment Langtree and his mystery companion stepped through the door at Stick's farewell party, every pair of eyes in the room lingered on her in open appraisal. It wasn't immediately clear who she was to him; the way she clung to him implied some sort of couplehood, but on the other hand, they were both gingers, which suggested at least an outside chance they were just siblings. She looked to be a few years older than Langtree—maybe twenty-six, twenty-seven—and pretty, even though, aside from her Dixie Chicks t-shirt, she was dressed about a decade out of date: big-ish hair, acid-washed jeans and denim jacket, clean white Reebok high-tops. Maybe a little on the curvy side. She eyeballed them all right back, her mouth a little curl of skepticism, appearing not the least bit intimidated by the roomful of close-knit, tipsy strangers. Meanwhile Langtree just stood next to her, smirking, like he was waiting to be announced at Buckingham Palace.

"I have never been so *cold* in my en-*tire life*," the mystery woman said to him. She wrapped both arms around his bicep and clung tight.

"New England gets cold, all right," Langtree said with a shrug.

"I'm gonna need a new coat for sure," she went on. "I wish I'd got one back in Texas. They're probably so expensive here."

"Come on," he said, and he grabbed her by the wrist and pulled her along behind him, toward the bar. "Let's get us some drinks."

The party was at The Approach, an unremarkable little bar on an otherwise empty stretch of highway between New Bedford and Cape Cod, one of five or six local bars that had yet to ban the crew of the Coast Guard cutter *Stargazer* from the premises. There were keno machines in the corner, a low stage at the far end of the room, and a green-gray carpet covering most of the floor. Heavily lacquered light wood paneling ran the length of the walls. A long rectangular light hung from the ceiling off to one side, marking the spot where a pool table had once been. It was the kind of place where everything always felt a little sticky. It held maybe eighty people at most, but as the couple transected the crowd, there was no question in anyone's mind that Langtree's woman would stand out in a room five times the size. She had a certain magnetism, one that turned men's heads even if they couldn't quite articulate what it was about her that drew them in.

At the bar, Langtree ordered a couple drinks: Coors for him, Zima for her. He took a long pull from his bottle and nodded at a few of his shipmates, acknowledging their open stares. His smirk dug in even further, like it could crack his entire face wide open. Everyone wanted to know but nobody wanted to be the first to ask. Langtree liked that. He liked making them squirm a little.

It was Welch whose curiosity got the better of him first. "Hey Langtree," he called from his spot at the end of the bar. "Who ya got there?" A lifelong New Englander with a cartoonish Yankee inflection—*Hooyuh gawt theyah?*—Welch was only twenty-five but was already the old man of the *Stargazer's* deck department. He used to work the commercial fishing boats before switching sides and joining the Coast Guard a couple years earlier. Langtree knew this the same way everyone else did, which was that Welch never shut up about it.

Langtree drew another long sip from his beer before answering. "This here's Janine," he drawled eventually, and he snatched up her left hand and held it up for the room to see. A skimpy diamond, in line with the limits of a junior enlisted man's paycheck, glinted in the ring on her finger. "She's my wife."

"Heyyyyyyyy," Janine said. Her smile was big and broad and intended to project confidence, but her eyes held a certain wariness, like a rabbit wondering if the coyotes had picked up her scent. "*So* nice to finally meet you. Brock simply did *not* stop talking about y'all on the drive up. For three whole days!"

In the brief time they'd been married, Langtree had already noticed Janine sometimes told obvious lies when she was nervous. Talking nonstop for three solid days would have been laughably out of character for him. He'd have sooner bought a pair of Birkenstocks at the outlet mall and worn them to a poetry reading. Still, it didn't bother him, and he wasn't about to correct her in front of other people. Maybe he'd mention it to her one of these days. "Janine, meet the crew of the *Stargazer*," he said, sweeping his arm out in front of him. "Well, some of 'em, anyway."

"A *wife*," Welch said. He sounded genuinely surprised. "Well how about that. I didn't even know you were married."

"No reason you woulda, since up until about a week ago I wasn't," Langtree answered with a shrug. "Went home for Christmas, bumped into Janine, we got to talking, one thing led to another and, well, here we are now, I guess." He'd been rehearsing that line in his head up until the moment he pulled the truck into the lot out back. Janine was the older sister of his high school best friend; growing up, the age difference between them was enough to keep them out of each other's social circles, but they had always been friendly. Before he saw her behind the bar at The Corner Pocket nineteen days ago, he hadn't seen her in years, not since her brother's funeral. He didn't even recognize her at first.

"Brock Langtree, as I live and breathe," she said, and he knew right away who she was. He hadn't realized until that moment, but something about her voice had imprinted on his brain back when he was around twelve years old. He felt his heart take a quick extra step. "Where the hell you been hiding yourself?" After that, everything happened so fast—the greedy first sex in the cab of his truck; the giddy rush of new plans for a shared future; the hungover, bleary-eyed, early morning courthouse visit, him in a suit pilfered from his father's closet the night before, her in a leftover bridesmaid's dress from an ex-best friend's wedding. The way she turned her face up to him and smiled as she squinted in the wintry sunshine on the courthouse steps afterwards, how with just that look she made him feel like he finally mattered to someone—well, he knew he'd carry that moment with him forever. *How'd I get so lucky,* he said, or maybe he only thought it because she didn't say anything, just leaned into him for protection from the wind. He would never admit it to Janine, but he couldn't quite remember whose idea the whole thing even was. It didn't sound like one of his—acting on impulse had never been his thing—but it also didn't matter. He wanted it, then and now, even if he hadn't known until it was all upon him.

He had no intention of sharing any of those details with his shipmates. It was none of their business. Let them wonder. If it lent him an air of mystery in the process, so much the better.

"Sure, I can see it," Welch said. "I can see how she'd fall for a silver-tongued devil like you. You're so smooth, you can talk the toothpaste right back into the tube."

"What's he talking about, hon?" Janine asked.

"No idea." The muscles in Langtree's jaw twitched. His smirk vanished. People had been making fun of Langtree for one thing or another his entire life, so he was used to it by now. He didn't always get the joke, but he never failed to recognize when he was on the receiving end of one. And it still always burned him. "But I don't believe I care for it."

Welch slapped his hand on the bar and honked out a laugh. "Relax, boot. I'm just winding you up. Don't take it personal. I'm happy for you—we *all* are. See? Come on, people. Give it up for the happy couple!" Everyone around the bar applauded obediently and then crowded around. The guys shook Langtree's hand and clapped him on the back while the wives and girlfriends awkwardly shoulder-hugged Janine, welcoming this complete stranger to their sorority of convenience and necessity. "Looks like Santa was good to you this year, brother."

"Oh, I reckon I've had worse Christmases," Langtree said, his knowing grin in full flower again. No sooner were the words out of his mouth than Janine grabbed his head with both hands and planted a forceful kiss squarely onto his lipless mouth. Caught off guard, he took an instinctive half-step back before he realized what was happening and allowed himself to just sink into it. Now this truly *was* out of character. Public displays of affection had always made him uncomfortable; even their first kiss as an official married couple had been modest and brief. But this was different. It was a party, though, so why the hell not, right? Langtree could feel the guys watching them the whole time, and he knew not a single one of them would have turned down the chance to swap places with him just then. Janine was sultry in a way the local women just weren't.

Then she broke off the kiss as suddenly as she started it and sucked down half her Zima in one go. "Baby, I wanna dance," she said. Stick's band was onstage now, cranking out some angsty suburban alt-rock song that had been all over the radio the previous summer. Janine's eyes were wide and eager, her mouth in a half-open, anticipating smile. She reminded Langtree of a puppy who had just heard the jangling sound of her leash in her master's hand. "Come on and dance with me."

"Naw, that's okay," Langtree said, and suddenly heat flashed across the back of his neck as the acute feeling of awkwardness that always accompanied being the center of attention shot through every nerve ending in his body.

"Don't be like that, baby," she cooed. "*Dance* with me."

"I don't know how to dance to this stuff."

"There's more to life than two-steppin', hon. Come on and lemme show you. *Pleeease.*"

"You go ahead and I'll be along presently," he said. "I think I'm gonna have a couple drinks with the guys first."

"Uh huh," she said. "All right. But if you're not out there in five minutes, mister, well, let's just say I can't be held responsible for what might happen." And she kissed him again before beelining to a spot smack in front of the stage. Langtree watched as she started to dance. She wasn't moving the way his shipmates were—they all looked like a gang of methed-up frat boys bouncing around out there, whereas Janine knew what she was doing. Where to find the groove, how to channel the music through her body, how to use the movements of her limbs, her shoulders, her hips to radiate something deeply alluring, sensual, and maybe even a little smutty out to the whole damn room.

"Damn, Langtree," Ocampo said. He handed Langtree a shot of tequila. "That's some kind of woman you got there."

"Yeah, you're gonna wanna hold onto that one," Welch chimed in. He raised his glass. "To the happy couple."

"Thanks," Langtree said. He downed his shot. The cheap liquor burned his throat; tequila wasn't his usual pour, but it felt rude to refuse it. He was still the new guy.

He still had to earn his way in. You didn't do that by turning down drinks. Then another appeared on the bar in front of him. He hadn't asked for this one either. He knocked it back. Then a third. This one didn't burn quite so much.

"Drink up, you poor bastard." This was Muñoz now. He slid yet another shot across the bar. "The night is young."

"I think I better slow down," Langtree said. The room was starting to wobble, and his words were bunching up in his mouth. "My wife's expecting me on the dance floor."

"Relax," Ocampo said. "She's not going anywhere. Don't worry so much."

Langtree lifted the shot glass to his lips.

When he woke up, he was lying on the floor in a pitch-dark room, with no memory of how he got there. The floor was cool and a little damp; it smelled like a hold full of rotting fish in there. Men's room, he thought. Beer before liquor. You'll never be sicker.

The room was spinning around him, which meant he was still drunk and therefore probably hadn't been in there too long. He thought about sitting up for a while before he tried it. When he finally did, he immediately regretted moving at all. Then he threw up in the sink. Nothing but stomach acid came up.

I'm up now, he thought. Hard part's over. He tried the door, only to find it locked from the outside.

"Hey," he croaked. His throat was raw; his mouth tasted wretched. Who locked the door? And where was Janine? Why hadn't she let him out? He pounded his fist on the door and rattled the doorknob. "Hey, got-dammit, lemme outta here!"

After a few minutes of this, the door opened. It was the bartender. Behind her, the drummer and the guitar player were in the middle of packing up their gear and rolling it out to the parking lot. The bar was almost completely empty. "Holy shit, you're alive," she said. "I was starting to wonder if you were ever gonna wake up."

"What the hell happened?"

The bartender shrugged. "I was busy. Your buddies can really put it away, you know that? All I know is, someone told me you were passed out in here so I locked the door for you. People were still going in and I didn't think you'd appreciate getting pissed on or whatever. Anyway, you've been in here for like three hours, and I've been holding it in for the last hour and a half. So if you don't mind?"

"Ain't there a ladies' room here?" Langtree asked.

She scowled. "Ever been *in* there? It's disgusting. Worse than any men's room I ever saw."

Out in the parking lot, the rear doors of the band's van were open. Janine and Stick were sitting inside, sharing a cigarette. Her legs dangled over the rear bumper. Langtree had never seen Janine smoke before. He saw Stick lean in and say something quietly into Janine's ear. She laughed, then looked up and saw him approaching.

"Where'd you get off to?" she asked. "I was looking for you."

"I'm gonna go see if the guys need any help," Stick said, and he went back into the bar. Langtree watched him go.

"Your hair's a hot mess," he said once Stick was back inside.

"I took a nap," she said. "In the truck, I mean."

"Uh huh." Her second obvious lie of the night. He fished around in his pocket and pulled out his keys. "I don't see how."

"You left it unlocked, you big dingus. I couldn't find you. Nobody knew where you were. I got tired of waiting."

"Uh huh." He wanted to take her at her word, he really did. But what if he was wrong? Word would get around. He'd become a walking joke, the dumb shitkicker who was in such a goddamn hurry that he married a wild woman he barely knew and couldn't hope to control. Nobody on the ship would ever take him seriously.

"Nothing happened, you know," she said. Langtree heard a defiant edge in her voice. "We were just talking."

"I don't believe you," he said.

◆

Later in life, on those infrequent occasions when Janine would think back on her time in New Bedford, her mind would always call up the way it looked when Langtree first brought her there: bleak, the sky a gray sheet stretched tight, the wind whipping off the water, the sharp smell of sewage and rot wafting in from the harbor. Shuttered storefronts and struggling businesses. Anonymous flat-fronted clapboard buildings, painted various shades of white or pale blue, all of which had seen better days. Cracked windows and rusting chain-link fences. The entire city sagging under the weight of its troubles. And no one looked happy.

"What kind of place did you bring me to?" she asked Langtree. They were in the truck, still a couple miles to go to their new one-bedroom apartment on the base, but she'd already seen enough.

"I know it ain't Texas," he said. "It just looks a lot worse than it is. You'll see."

Janine fumed for the next mile or two, but there really wasn't much she could say. Before she married Langtree, the furthest from Bronough, Texas—population 1,374—she'd ever been was Oklahoma City, for church camp one year, not nearly far enough. For most of her life, she'd dreamed of getting the hell out and never looking back, of living a life where people weren't perfectly willing to stab you in the back so long as it holds off the ever-encroaching boredom just a little longer. But there weren't many roads leading out of Bronough. So when Langtree offered her a ticket out, she grabbed it, both hands, no hesitation. Would she have gone with him if she hadn't actually loved him? She'd spent the whole drive asking herself that very question. She didn't think so. But she hoped he wouldn't ask her directly, because she couldn't be sure of the answer she might give.

Langtree told her how New Bedford used to be a big fishing town until about fifteen or twenty years before. Boats would go out for a week or two and come back with holds filled to bursting with cod, flounder, haddock. The money just kept flowing in, a tide no one thought would ever recede. But eventually it did recede, when the fisheries ran out of fish, and then that tide dragged back everything it had ever given them.

It's why people in New Bedford hated Coasties so much, he went on. There were rules now, he said, rules the Coast Guard had to enforce about who could fish when and where and how much. Naturally, the fishermen resented them for it. A lot of them had had to switch cargo, from haddock to heroin, just to hang onto their boats.

This was all news to Janine. "So what does that mean?" she asked. "Do I gotta watch my back when I go out for groceries?"

"Just keep to the other wives and stay away from the townies," he said. "You'll be fine."

Langtree spent the first week of domesticated life brooding about the incident at The Approach. He never said a word about it either way, but Janine could tell. He wasn't so hard to read. *Ugh*, that stupid party. It pained her to even think about, especially since the whole mess had been so avoidable—she knew how her meds sometimes reacted to booze. It had happened before, and she was usually more careful about mixing the two. Still, there was nothing anyone could do about it now. Best not to dwell. She wondered if Langtree planned to go on brooding for the next three and a half weeks, right up until the day the *Stargazer* was scheduled to get underway again. Janine was already a little eager to be rid of him, though she never said so out loud. Maybe a month and a half at sea would help adjust his perspective. It wasn't as if they'd been together so long that he should need a reminder of why he married her.

On the other hand, his impending departure meant she would soon be all by herself, alone in a place as foreign to her as Picadilly Circus.

Well, that was all right. She'd manage just fine on her own. She always had.

The day before the *Stargazer* left port, Langtree brought Janine home a surprise.

"I never asked for this," she said.

"His name's Roscoe," Langtree said of the dog at the end of the leash he was holding. "But I reckon you can still change it if you want. Woman at the shelter said he's only three months or so."

Janine looked down at Roscoe, a brown and white boxer with paws the size of shovel blades and a tail whipping back and forth like a switch. The dog stopped sniffing around the kitchen for a moment and looked back at her, his expression expectant but patient, as if he knew she was making up her mind about him and was doing his best to make a good impression. *Goddammit.* This was the last thing she needed. "We never talked about this," she said. "What if I was allergic?"

"You ain't, though," he said. "I know that much."

"That's not the point. I'm not even a dog person. Why did you think I'd want one? Especially with you about to be gone?"

"That's exactly why right there. You need something to keep you company. Give you a reason to get out of bed in the morning."

That's what the pills are for, she almost said. "I've been getting myself outta bed my whole life," she shot back instead. "I don't see why I'd need this dog to help me with that all of a sudden."

"No reason, I guess," he said after a pause. "I guess I'm just the worrying kind."

Back at Bruno County Regional High School, Janine had always been one of the popular girls, or at least that's the way she had come to remember it. In those days, she never had to seek social approval from others; *they* sought it from *her*. But now she was the newcomer, trying to ingratiate herself with an alien and long-established clique: the cabal of *Stargazer* wives.

She did her best. Many of them had similar names— there was a Kristen and a Kristy and a Kiersten, and a Kim and a Kimberly—and several had small children. Janine was not interested in children, never did have any patience for them, and she had difficulty masking her irritation when these kids got fussy during a wives' outing. These women had all spent a large part of their adult lives in this sequestered little subculture. They shared the same secret language and a deep catalogue of cultural references and inside jokes that would take Janine months to learn. They let her hang out with them for a week or so, but eventually all but one of them stopped returning her calls.

Janine understood what was happening well enough. Their initial acceptance had been only out of politeness. In reality they resented her, for her Texas twang and her attire and her sudden imposition upon them, or for what they probably assumed had gone on between her and

Stick in the parking lot, or for the way their husbands had been sneaking looks at her that night, or for Langtree's unspoken assumption they would automatically accept her simply because she was there. And even if they ever did, she knew it would come with an asterisk: to this little coterie of lifelong New Englanders, Janine would always be The Other, the token Texan. And there was nothing she could do about it.

The only one who continued to hang out with Janine was Rochelle. Rochelle was from somewhere in far northern New Hampshire. She was short and round and she dressed almost exclusively in New England Patriots jerseys and sweatshirts. Her manners were a bit on the rough side, and she wasn't the easiest person to hold a conversation with, but Janine knew she was in no position to be choosy. Besides, they both liked the same music, which was at least something. Janine had built friendships on less. So she kept calling.

Their first outing was to the mall, for lunch at Ruby Tuesday. Their table was along the side of the restaurant that was open to the rest of the mall. Janine ordered a disappointing southwestern chicken salad. Rochelle ordered a cheeseburger and then spent most of the meal making snide remarks about the shoppers who passed within earshot of them.

"Check out the life skills master over there with the unlit cigarette in his mouth," she said halfway through her second margarita. She nodded at a man passing the Sunglass Hut directly across from them. "Like he can't even wait til he's in the parking lot to gratify that oral fixation." The man shot them both a fiery look.

"I think he heard you," Janine whispered. Still on her first margarita, she was already finding it hard to keep her mind focused.

"What's he gonna do about it? Nothing, that's what." Rochelle downed the remainder of her drink and signaled the waiter. "Ready for another," she said. She nodded at Janine. "What about you?"

Janine held up her glass. "Still workin' on this one, thanks."

"I never woulda pegged you for a lightweight. Not after Stick's party, anyway. Oh, man," she said, her gaze now fixed on a short, muscular man strutting by in tight white jeans, black high-tops, and a turquoise Member's Only jacket. "Check *this* out."

"It's a statement, I'll give him that," Janine offered.

Rochelle honked. "He walks like he's got a stick up his ass and his balls are too heavy." Then she fished her phone out of her purse, flipped it open, and started pressing buttons. "Hang on, this'll be real quick."

Janine wondered how Rochelle could afford it: Rochelle's husband was a paygrade higher than Langtree, but even with that modest bump, a phone plan would still be a stretch for them just now.

The phone had become a constant presence whenever Janine and Rochelle went out, whether it was for bowling, getting their nails done, or that day trip into Boston. With each outing, Rochelle would spend more and more of their time together on her phone, contributing mostly monosyllabic responses to their conversation as she sent and received a steady stream of text messages. It annoyed Janine, but she did her best to keep it hidden. It wasn't as if she had a lot of other options.

"I think I've seen more movies these last couple of weeks with you than I have over the last two years," Janine said one afternoon, hoping to draw Rochelle out a bit and cement the friendship with a little chit-chat. They were having ice cream at Friendly's, after a matinee screening of *The Matrix*.

"Lotta good movies out right now," Rochelle said. She slurped down a spoonful of vanilla ice cream, whipped cream, and Reese's Pieces before the words were even out of her mouth.

"I guess," Janine said. "I don't know. I don't really think I understood this one."

Rochelle paused her shoveling for a moment and raised her eyebrows. "Seriously?"

Something in Rochelle's expression put Janine on the defensive. So damn smug and patronizing, like she thought she was hot shit on a silver platter. Janine tried to keep the hurt out of her tone but didn't quite manage it. "Did *you* understand it?"

"Of course," Rochelle said with a snort. "What's so confusing about it?"

Janine sighed. She felt a headache coming on. "I don't know. All of it, I guess. Maybe sci-fi just isn't my thing. My mind always wanders."

Rochelle shook her head and sniggered under her breath. Then she reached into her purse, took out her phone and sent another text. A couple seconds later, it beeped in reply, and she barked out a sharp *haw*.

That was the last straw.

"You know," she said, "I haven't said anything up to now, but I need to tell you that I find it extremely rude when you do that." Her voice was shot through with exasperation and pique, but all of a sudden she didn't give a damn about that.

Rochelle cocked her head and leaned back, like a chicken, eyes wide with surprise. "Excuse me?"

"You are always on that dang phone when we're supposed to be hanging out," Janine said. Her back was well and truly up now, and even though she recognized she was almost certain to damage, possibly irreparably, the one friendship she had going here, she couldn't stop herself. All the frustrations of her life—Rochelle, Brock, that dog, the weather, the rest of those idiot wives, everyone's need to judge her all the damn time, *all* of it— were suddenly bursting forth all at once, clamoring to shove their way through the narrow fissure Janine had just cracked open. "I'm trying to have a pleasant conversation with you, and you're somewhere else. You're *always* somewhere else. What am I supposed to think about that?" A woman with her two very young children in the next booth looked over at them, and Janine realized she must have been getting a bit loud. She didn't care about that either.

"I mean, it seems pretty obvious to me," Rochelle said with a shrug.

"Well why don't you spell it out for me, then."

Rochelle paused. Her expression suggested she was trying to figure out exactly how serious Janine was. Janine steeled herself for the worst. Then Rochelle shrugged, bit down on her straw, and slurped up the dregs of her Coke. "Okay," she said finally. "Well, I guess I might as well tell you. The deal is, Ronnie told me to keep an eye on you while the ship's out. He said it was your husband's idea."

"How do you mean, exactly?" Janine asked, but she already knew the answer. "Keep an eye on me, as in, make sure I have what I need and I'm settling in okay?"

"No," Rochelle said. "The other way."

Janine could not quite process what she was hearing. Her insides tightened. She felt like she'd just taken a kickball to the solar plexus, as though her body was about to reject the ice cream she'd been eating like it would a bad kidney, like everything anyone she'd ever trusted had told her about the world was not just wrong, but an intentional, malicious lie. She felt like a goddamn sucker.

"Ronnie's gonna be so pissed," Rochelle went on. "I wasn't supposed to say anything."

"No," Janine squeaked. "No way. I don't believe you."

"Fine. You're right. He didn't. I made it up. Now we can just drop it."

But Janine knew it was true. It was the missing piece that finally made sense of the whole puzzle. I could just kick myself, she thought, and then she realized she couldn't work out whose betrayal hurt more. "But . . . now wait, I don't understand," she said. "I mean, why—"

Rochelle smacked her bowl with her spoon. The sound of it echoed through the mostly empty restaurant. "Oh my *god*. Why do you think? Because of Stick. *Jesus*. Is everyone in Texas this slow?"

Janine's eyes began to water up. She felt her breath start to hitch on its way out. "Well then. I guess now I know why you kept returning my calls when no one else did," she said. She focused her gaze on the cash register on the other side of the restaurant. She didn't trust herself to hold it together if she looked at Rochelle directly. "I have never been so humiliated in my life. I hope you're pleased with yourself, I really do. My god. I cannot *believe* I thought we were friends. I'm such an *idiot*."

"I don't exactly feel good about it, you know," Rochelle snapped. "This hasn't been easy for me either."

"So sorry for your troubles." Janine stood to leave. She was so close to tears now, and the last thing she wanted was for Rochelle to see them. Even hiccup-crying in the car, pathetic as it would be, seemed more dignified. "Thanks so much for another lovely afternoon," she called over her shoulder as she hurried out.

Later that evening, alone in the darkening apartment, Janine drank her last beer and flipped through her mental rolodex of regrets. Losing it in front of Rochelle, who didn't deserve to know the first goddamn thing about her, let alone see her at her most vulnerable. Marrying a man she barely knew, for reasons she couldn't even begin to explain—a man who was completely unreachable for six weeks at a stretch, no less. Giving Stick so much as the time of day back at his stupid party. Leaving the desperate but familiar existence she'd known her whole life. Believing life could get better. Believing she even deserved that.

Is this the way it's always gonna be now? Unlike a lot of her friends growing up, Janine had never spent a whole lot of time imagining what married life would be like, mostly because she didn't expect to experience it. But she never would have guessed it would be as isolating as this.

She could always leave. Just get in his truck and drive away somewhere. That's what her momma would've told her to do for sure. *Girl, why waste precious hours of your short life in a place you don't wanna be,* she'd have said. He wouldn't even know about it for weeks. But Janine knew the idea was a non-starter as soon as it occurred to her. It wasn't like there was any money to fund another fresh start, so soon after the first one. And besides, where was she gonna go? Back to Texas? No *thank* you. *The only way forward is forward* was another thing her momma liked to say, and this was about as much forward as Janine could manage just now.

But even if she'd had money and a place to go, she knew she'd most likely just stay put. On the surface, the Brock Langtree who had emerged in New Bedford seemed not to be the same one she remembered—he'd always been quiet and reserved, but the old Langtree had a certain sweetness to him, a softness perhaps borne of his self-appointed role as human barricade between his father and kid brother. She'd heard about that from Jake, her brother; even in those days, Langtree would never have let on about his own troubles. He probably still had no idea she knew.

Maybe the years between then and now had made him hard somehow. It was a common enough affliction among the men in their part of the world. But he wasn't like them. And as grateful as she was for that, she knew how difficult it had made things for him growing up: he *wasn't* one of them, and they never let him forget it.

And that's how she knew the sweet and awkward boy who used to fix up dirtbikes and race them with her little brother out behind the high school and the sullen, sulking man she'd married were still one and the same. The light had to be just right, and you maybe had to squint a little, but you could see it plain as day if you knew how to look.

She looked down at Roscoe, curled up at her feet. His paws twitched as he slept, chasing rabbits through his dreams.

"Roscoe, you poor dumb bastard," she sighed. "What am I gonna do now?"

One thing she could do—get herself a new doctor who'd take her off them damn pills. They'd already wrecked more than they fixed.

◆

The *Stargazer* returned to New Bedford a few days before Easter, which seemed auspicious to Langtree. What better time to resurrect his marriage—or at least revive it from life support—than during the celebration of the eternal life granted to those who believe?

It had taken him some time to come around to this perspective. He'd spent the first few weeks of the patrol making contingency plans for a quick and dirty divorce. He may not have known exactly what happened between his wife and Stick, but he knew enough. After speaking with both the ship's yeoman and the legal assistance officer, he decided to head up to the district headquarters office in Boston once the *Stargazer* was in port again and talk to one of the legal aid lawyers they had there, who knew how divorce worked in Massachusetts.

"They get guys like you in there all the time," the yeoman said, sensing Langtree's reluctance. "Do you have any idea how many Coastie marriages fail? It's a lot, I'm telling you. And a lot more of 'em *should* fail. Mine included."

It made sense, really. It was for the best. They could both just walk away from what was, in retrospect, an obvious mistake and start over fresh. They were still young enough. Langtree's sour mood brightened almost overnight.

Langtree wasn't the sort to openly discuss his personal business, but somehow the entire crew seemed to know what he'd decided. Many of them volunteered their opinions, which were almost uniformly that he should dump the bitch, because a cheater was a cheater, and also she wasn't really all that hot anyway.

The only dissenter was January, one of the cooks. He stopped Langtree on the flight deck one day, while Langtree was doing his rounds.

"If you ask me," he said, "you should forget about it. Just let it go."

"I didn't ask, though," Langtree said. "In fact, I don't recall asking any of you people a damn thing."

"Oh I know. I'm telling you anyway. You need to hear this, whether you know it or not." He took a long draw on his cigarette. Langtree, who'd quit smoking just after high school, breathed deep the secondhand smoke. He would have killed for a tin of dip just then. "Listen. I've been married almost fifteen years now, which averages out to around five years per wife. I've been through a lot, including a couple of times very similar to what's going on with you right now."

There wasn't anyone on the ship Langtree trusted, exactly, but January might have come the closest. There was an earnestness and openness about him that resonated with Langtree. January never seemed to want anything from anyone. Langtree decided to hear him out.

"All right," he said. "So what'd you do about it?"

"That's not important," January said quickly. "What *is* important is how I felt *later*, when I had time to look back and reflect about my own actions and reactions and whatnot. And do you know how I felt? Go ahead, guess."

"I wouldn't know," Langtree said.

"Like a goddamn fool, is how. See, I let my *pride* get in my way." He jabbed Langtree three or four times in the chest with his index finger. "I had a lot of pride in those days. Long story short, my pride was hurt, and that hurt blinded me to what I had and what I was doing. By the time I figured that out, it was too late."

Langtree's face soured. "A man without pride ain't much of a man, though."

January laughed. "Exactly what I'd expect a cowboy like you to say," he said. "Maybe you're right. Who knows. But think about this. What *is* pride, anyway? What's even the point of it? My whole life, pride never kept me warm for even one single night. Pride isn't what gave me my two beautiful daughters. So sure, you can keep on acting out of pride, but all you'll be in the end is alone in a room, with nothing to keep you company but your stupid pride." He ground out the cigarette and wiped his hands down the front of his chef's whites. "You're the only one can decide if that's worth it."

Langtree stood on the flight deck and thought about it for a while after January left and concluded it was not.

He had married Janine for a reason. It was a reason he could not quite express through language but nevertheless felt deep in his core. That feeling had gone dormant since their arrival in New Bedford, but now it seemed to have flared back to life, as robust as it had been on their wedding day. Imagining what might have happened between her and Stick turned his stomach, but it did nothing to tamp the flame. He suddenly regretted not calling her when the ship had stopped in Key West; he did try once, but hung up when he heard the answering machine click on. He'd meant to try again, but he just couldn't seem to get his thoughts lined up properly for a conversation in the confinement of that little phone booth. So he didn't.

The *Stargazer* arrived pierside at a little before three in the afternoon. A throng of family members milled about the pier and parking lot, waiting for all the fathers and husbands to spill over the gangway, finally home after six long weeks of separation. Langtree was a linehandler up on the forecastle, right at the bow of the ship, and was always one of the last of the crew to secure from special sea detail and be officially granted liberty. When he finally made it onto dry land, Janine was not there to greet him.

Maybe nobody called her. Had Langtree added their number to the *Stargazer* phone tree list before he left? He couldn't remember.

He ended up getting a lift home from Dixon. Langtree could see from a block away that his truck wasn't in the driveway—Janine wasn't at home either. Inside, the house was clean and smelled of cinnamon. Except for the new DVD player on top of the television, the place was mostly how Langtree remembered it. He shook his head. Those machines cost a couple hundred bucks easy, even down at the Wal-Mart. Glad to see she's been taking good care of herself, he thought. Maybe she kept the receipt.

It took Langtree a couple minutes to notice the other difference in the house. Roscoe was nowhere to be found. There was no dog bed, no bowl, no squeaky toys. It was like he'd never been there at all.

Langtree went to the bedroom and opened the closet. Janine's clothes were all still inside. Her suitcase was on the shelf above the hanging rod, exactly where she'd put it on the day they moved in, not even three months ago.

So. She still lived there, at least. That was something.

He availed himself of one of the beers in the fridge and settled in to wait. He put on one of the DVDs Janine had brought home sometime over the last few weeks—it was *Mrs. Doubtfire*—even though he'd just seen it a couple of weeks ago; they had it in the ship's movie locker. He let his mind wander as the movie played. Outside, the daylight began to fade. Inside, Langtree didn't move to turn on a light, letting the house slowly darken.

He kept circling back to his conversation with January. He had felt so certain in his decision immediately afterward, but now? He wasn't so sure anymore. Maybe his first instinct had been the right one—he'd always been the type who made decisions quickly and never looked back, never second-guessed himself. And now here he was, second-guessing his second guess. Maybe January had just caught him in a vulnerable moment. Maybe he just didn't want to be alone.

Around seven o'clock, headlights swept across the living room window and pulled Langtree out of his nap. He heard the sound of his truck outside, the familiar purring of its engine. Then it went quiet, and a moment later Janine walked through the front door.

"Oh good," she said as she put her purse down on the kitchen table. "You got a ride home. I was worried."

Langtree got up from the couch and went into the kitchen. Janine was rummaging through the fridge. "I'll tell you what, I am just about starving right now," she said. "All I had today was a tiny bowl of Fruit Loops and half a sandwich. You eat yet? I could maybe fix us something."

"I wasn't sure you still lived here," he said.

She brought her head out of the fridge. "What's that, now?"

"I said, I wasn't sure you still lived here."

"Don't be ridiculous. Why wouldn't I?" She poked her head back into the fridge and shortly emerged with a box of fried chicken, which she gently shook. "Jackpot—there's still four or five pieces in here. You want in on this?"

Langtree ignored the leftovers. She was trying to distract him, he knew that, but his stomach was a tight tangle of nerves. He couldn't have eaten a single bite even if he wanted to, which he didn't because nobody in New England knew the right way to fry up a damn chicken anyway. "You tell me," he said. "You didn't pick me up. You weren't here when I got home."

"I know, and I really am sorry about that." She turned her back to Langtree and dumped the chicken pieces onto a plate. "But I couldn't get anyone to cover my shift."

"Shift?" Well, that explained the DVD player, anyway. "You got a job now? Since when?"

"Since about three weeks ago. Bartending down at Jimmy Conners'."

Langtree knew the place. It was on Union Street, one of those brass-and-fern bars catering to what was left of New Bedford's downtown professional crowd. It could have been worse: at least it wasn't Dave's Aqua Lounge or, god forbid, The National. Still. They hadn't even talked about her working at all. "What do you need with a job?" he asked.

"What the hell else am I supposed to do while you're gone for six weeks at a time?" She shoved the plate into the microwave and slammed the door. "Besides, we need the money. I've seen your paystubs. We ain't getting very far on those, sorry to say."

She was right about that; in the lightheadedness of those early days, he hadn't even thought about how he was going to support a whole other person on what he earned. He considered acknowledging this, as a way of defusing the situation before it got away from him completely. "That's why I got you that dog," he said instead. "Keep you company. Where *is* Roscoe, anyway?"

"I told you," she said slowly. "I didn't want to take care of any dog. I told you that the day you brought him home."

"That ain't no kind of answer. And come on, turn around and face me when you're talking to me."

"Fine." Janine whirled around and folded her arms in one efficient motion. She fixed Langtree with a chilling stare. It was clinical and piercing and uncomfortable as hell, but what worried him more than the stare itself was that he couldn't quite identify what was going on just behind it.

"Well I'm sorry to be the one to tell you this, but the fact is, Roscoe ran off. I put him out back while I was cooking dinner. He musta jumped that fence when I wasn't looking."

Oh you got to be kidding me. "Dammit, Janine," he said. "How the hell did you let that happen?"

She held up a hand and shook her head. "This is not my fault," she said. "Don't you try to blame me. I told you. I *told* you."

"Well hell. I mean, did you look for him, at least?"

"Of course I looked for him. What kind of person do you think I am? I put up signs and everything."

Langtree frowned. Something about this wasn't lining up quite right. "And no one found him, brought him back," he mused. "And he never came back on his own, either."

Janine spread her arms wide. "He ain't here, is he?"

"Mmmm," he said, and suddenly he was imagining himself as the prosecutor on some courtroom TV drama, about to pounce on the fatal flaw in the guilty man's alibi and expose his lies for the whole world to see. He tried not to smile. "See, what I'm wondering is, why *wouldn't* he come back?"

"What do you mean?"

"Well, his *food's* here. His *bed's* here. Or they *were*, anyway. You sure got rid of his stuff awful quick."

"I couldn't say," she said. The microwave pinged behind her. She ignored it. "I don't think like a dog. Probably someone found him and kept him."

"But he had tags," Langtree persisted. "You got him his tags like I told you, right?"

"Or maybe he got hit by a car," she went on. "How should I know?"

"But someone woulda looked at his tags and got in touch with you." Janine dropped her gaze to the floor. "He didn't have his tags, did he?"

"I mean, he had his collar on."

"Got-dammit, Janine. You were supposed to get him his papers. Like I told you. Now he's gone for good." A powerful and surprising despondency washed over him. He barely even knew this dog; why was he feeling this loss so acutely? He let out a long sigh and rubbed his eyes. "We ain't never gonna see that dog again because of you."

And just like that, Janine was all up in his face. "Listen," she said, her index finger almost touching Langtree's nose. "I *know* why you got me that dog. Don't think for a minute I don't. It was the same reason you had your buddy's wife pretend to be my friend so she could spy on me. So you could control me while you were away."

"Whoa, whoa, whoa. Hold up a sec. I never—"

"Stop. Just stop. Rochelle told me everything, okay? So I know. I know *all* of it."

Shit. He'd known it was a risky idea when Ronnie first suggested it; Langtree didn't know Rochelle at all, but Ronnie swore she could keep her mouth shut. Well, so much for *that*. That's what you get for trusting people. "It wasn't like that," he said, and then thought better of it. "Well, I guess maybe it was. But you can't blame—"

"Don't you *even*," she snapped, and he could tell from the fury in her eyes how serious she was. "If you know what's good for you, just *don't*."

They stood there, just inches apart, in total silence for four or five deep breaths before Janine pulled a chair from the table and dropped herself into it.

"I didn't mean for that dog to escape, but he did," she said. "I'm sorry I lost your property. Am I crying over the fact that he's gone? I am not. And I'll tell you what else, I believe I would have been well within my rights to take him right back to the dang shelter where you got him. But I didn't. Wouldn't be fair to the dog, now would it? Wasn't his fault you decided to use him the way you did."

"No, I guess not," Langtree mumbled.

"As for his stuff? I got rid of it because I just didn't want to be reminded."

"That he was gone?"

"No," she said. "Of why he was here in the first place." She leaned back in her chair. Langtree recognized the expression on her face immediately. It was the same one she'd had on that night at The Approach, the dubious, appraising mask that always made whoever was on the other end of it feel like she was toting up their every character flaw, every mistake they ever made, every wrong they ever did to another human being. "I never would have expected this from you," she went on. "Never in my life. What else don't I know, Brock? You got any other surprises for me? Hidden cameras tucked away somewhere? Something like that?"

"No," he said. He knew she was right. He had wronged her deeply, and had no defense to offer. He was utterly depleted. "Nothing else."

"So. You come home and the first thing we do is fight. That can't be a good sign."

"I reckon we got some things to sort out."

"Yep, I reckon we do," she said. "I reckon we do. So what does this mean? Where're we at now? You and me, I mean."

Langtree closed his eyes and drummed his fingertips on the particle board tabletop. Moment of truth time. All he had to do was say the words, recite the incantation that would release them both: *I think we made a mistake.* That's what he'd wanted weeks ago, and now here she was offering it up to him like so much leftover fried chicken. All he had to do was grab it.

And yet. *And yet.*

He opened his eyes and said, "I gotta know."

"Know what?"

"You know what," he said. "I gotta know what happened."

"Oh please," she said. "That again."

"We can talk about the other stuff too," he continued. "I owe you an apology, I know it. Maybe we can get past all this and maybe we can't. But I won't know that until I know the one thing I need to know about."

Janine looked at him for a long time. She wanted to peer all the way to his soul and then beyond even that, down to the unknowable germ at the core of his personhood, so she could finally catch a glimpse—even for a fraction of a fraction of a second—of who the man she married really was, of what the hell he really wanted. But it was no good. His eyes were completely impenetrable; all she could see in them was herself.

So that's the way it's gonna be, she thought. Then she stood up, went to the pantry, and came back with a bottle of warm vodka and two shot glasses.

"All right then," she said as she poured. An unexpected feeling of serenity settled in her, and she realized she'd been waiting for this as much as he had. *The only way forward was forward.* She smiled. "Where you wanna start?"

Spencer Fleury has worked as a sailor, copywriter, geography professor, and record store clerk, among other disreputable professions. His first novel, *How I'm Spending My Afterlife*, was reissued by Woodhall Press in 2021. He lives in San Francisco.

Acknowledgements

This book would not have been possible without the following people, places, and institutions:

Joshua Mohr, whose editorial guidance was instrumental in making these stories shine their brightest.

The members of the Bay Area Manuscript Group who workshopped these stories: Christina Robinson, Pam Squyres, Casey Bennett, Cyn Nooney, Jeremy Mann, Linda Hamilton, and Emily Bruenig.

The editors who saw fit to publish earlier versions of some of these stories: James Brubaker, Chris Hayes, Nate Knapp, Andrew Luft, Sara Novic, and W. Scott Olsen.

The places where I was able to grab a table and write these stories for hours on end without anyone kicking me out: In San Francisco, the Castro Writers' Co-op and Epicenter Coffee (you are both missed); in St. Petersburg, Florida, the main branch of the public library and the Starbucks on 4th Street North and 88th Ave North.

Jen Hayes, who makes everything possible for me.

And of course, Alan Good at Malarkey Books. Thanks for believing in this one.

Still Alive, a novel by LJ Pemberton
Hope and Wild Panic, stories by Sean Ennis
Sleep Decades, stories by Israel A. Bonilla
Thumbsucker, poems by Kat Giordano
The Great Atlantic Highway & Other Stories,
by Steve Gergley
First Aid for Choking Victims,
stories by Matthew Zanoni Müller

DEATH OF PRINT TITLES

Consumption & Other Vices, a novel by Tyler Dempsey
Awful People, a novel by Scott Mitchel May
Drift, a novel by Craig Rodgers
The Ghost of Mile 43, a novel by Craig Rodgers
One More Number, stories by Craig Rodgers
Francis Top's Grand Design, stories by Craig Rodgers
Francis Top's Lost Cipher, stories by Craig Rodgers

9 798990 324084